The Short of it All: Dreams and Scenes of Memoir Fiction

Marc Timmerman

Floricanto Press

Floricanto is a trademark of *Floricanto Press*.

Berkeley Press is an imprint of Inter-American Development, Inc.

Floricanto Press

7177 Walnut Canyon Rd.

Moorpark, California 93021

(415) 793-2662

www.*FloricantoPress*.com

ISBN-13: 978-1986065597

"Por nuestra cultura hablarán nuestros libros. Our books shall speak for our culture."

Roberto Cabello-Argandoña and Leyla Namazie, Editors

Cover Art: With permission, *Bird Dream* (detail) by © 2018 Gamaliel Ramírez, Chicago Boricúa artist.

Sit at your window and dream of the message when evening comes.

—Franz Kafka, "A Message from the Emperor"

For Esther,
For Nancy, Jeannette, Pilar, and Carlos
For their spouses and pets
For all our grandchildren
For Elaine, Joanne, Adrienne, Joanne and Samantha,
     spouses and pets
For Gamaliel Ramírez, friends and his family
For John and Gay
For all those who dream and live dreams and scenes...

$\mathcal{A}$cknowledgments

"A Bullied Boy's Dream" first appeared as a section of a story, "The Little Boy Who Flew Away," in my Stores of *Winter* (Santiago, Chile/Houston: Bravo y Allende/ LACASA, 2005).

"Dark Heaven, Dark Earth" is a modified version of a passage which first appeared in *Warman,* my adaptation of Georg Buchner's *Wozzeck* (unpublished, 1968).

The Venice section of "Paris and Venice" is adapted from "Menace in Venice," which first appeared in *The Italian Daze: Notes of a Lost Wanderer* (Moorpark, CA: Floricanto Press 2017).

"Return to Bellagio" first appeared as "Ritorno a Bellagio," in the Italian-language version of *The Italian Daze, La penisola non trovata I giorni italiani di un viandante perduto.* (Milano. Greco e Greco. April 2017).

"The Sculpture" is a slightly modified version of the story which was first published in *El Beisman* 2014-05-01. http://www.elbeisman.com/article.php?action=read&id=198, and then appeared in *Martín and Marvin: A Chicago Jewish Mexican, His Friend and Their Latin Worlds.* (Chicago. LACASA Chicago. 2016).

All other texts appear here for the first time.

Table of Contents

*I*ntroduction
Trivial Stories, Dreams, and Memoir Fictions

What is a trivial story? For M, it's a story that may have some spark and delight but leads to nothing profound, makes few demands on writer or reader but remains without any apparently enigmatic representation of something beyond itself. It's a way of telling things that doesn't scare writer or reader, allows him or her to go forward with the sensation that there's no risk, not much really at stake except maybe at times a somewhat artful telling. But in the end like all in life, there's deeper connection to other things, but that deeper connection would not surface if the intent were to find it clearly and directly. What emerges only does so as the result of a sleight of hand that projects the apparent intent not to find great meaning in stories even as such meaning may, at least sometimes, surface.

M wanted to write significant fiction, but he also wanted a life of significant adventures. One goal seemed to interfere with the other and he certainly didn't want to be a bore or live boringly, so he had to make his decision. But he tried to cheat, have his cake and eat it, as they say—though the why of it all was beyond him. And he had to face the fact that this very inability, lack or refusal of imagination marked his limit as a writer. To write significant fiction without imagination, one had to live a great, imaginative life.; and then refuse to betray what happened, have such special experience so that the mere recitation of what happened would lead to significant fiction. And that was his decision after all. But then how could one live a great life if one could or would not imagine anything?

The solution was to never say no, to throw oneself into the night, to refuse any break in the experiential flow, to quell any doubt or fear and go on. To say always yes to whatever came his way without holding back, without allowing fear or hesitation to govern him, to risk depravity and humiliation, to let others do what they would with him without a qualm or a moment's reluctance, to let one's life flow with its tides high and low, and then... naturally, and virtually without any imagination, to write about what had happened, just because what had happened was in itself worthy of imagining.

Such was the career he mapped out for his life and then his belated return to writing fiction. And for the most part he succeeded at least minimally. But then came the rub— first, some of the experiences were too painful to write about without re-living and perhaps even deepening that pain. But when he backed off and didn't tell the story because it was just too much to take, something else would happen—a dream would emerge, almost confused and confusing, difficult to remember and all but impossible to transcribe. But then sometimes it would be so vivid and pointed that, while he could only imperfectly remember what he 'd dreamt, he did have something to get down. It's true he often had to resort to his feeble imagination to finish a dream-story and make minimal

2

and yes perhaps somewhat trivial sense of what he dreamed. And these falsified dream stories would join his other small stories based on incidents and anecdotes of his life experience, to round out a body of work that could only be classified as "memoir fiction." And in many cases, *trivial* memoir fiction, at least according to some.

Of course, you could never really write pure memory anyway. Memory itself involves falsification because we can never fully evoke precisely what took place; our stored impressions are always distorted by what happened earlier in our lives as well as all the things that have happened after the sequence of events remembered. And then of course there is also the influence of existing literary patterns on what we presumably transcribe. But if remembrances are ultimately fiction, no matter how based on our experiences, then, memoirs are a kind of narrational representation of consciousness; and memoir fiction is the overt reworking of memory into an aesthetically refracted story. And of course, memoir dream fiction is somehow the narration of dream which, throughout or in one moment or another, requires the intervention, however poorly or trivially, of some fictional trope or move that gives what we can recall of our dreams the substance and form required to achieve status as a "literary work." Inevitably what results is not memoir but fiction, or "lying narrative" at best.

It is true M's imagination was substantially limited. He always had to start from what he experienced or dreamed. But it is also true that he had to magnify, color or otherwise transform his lived or imagined experiences or merely write the drabbest things. ...

This small book is one of dreams and scenes that are among the shorter works that have emerged from my pursuit of memoir fiction, over the last few years. Some perhaps at least seem to be quite trivial, others are apparently trying for more but probably don't make it, although I might add with all modesty that, taken together, some and maybe all of them do achieve some kind of ultimate depth. Some of the stories stem from boyhood memories and impressions; several stem from anxieties throughout a life as professor and writer—a life haunted time after time by the dread of being diminished, mocked or forgotten in a not so gentle rush toward the dark. The dark pervades and yet somehow illuminates the short as well as the long of it all.

These dreams and scenes are really "the short" of what I've written—really the short of my all.

$\mathscr{P}$rologue
The Out of Gas Triptych

1. Out of Gas

With a girlfriend seated behind him, M was riding on a motor bike, something quite unusual for him to be doing and maybe for her too. Soon enough the bike sputtered and choked to a halt, and he and his friend walked the bike here and there until they found what seemed to advertise itself as a gas station. But when they approached the place it looked like its gas-pumping days were over, and that their search was for naught. Still they decided to enter what somehow even appeared to be a store if nothing else— "Nothing ventured, nothing gained," M observed. And there they found three men huddled over a card table, deeply engrossed in a game of poker, and none too interested in the two potential customers who'd walked through their door. They played out their hand and only then did one of the men, a surly cracker barrel type, who, it soon became clear, owned the place, turned toward them and asked how he might oblige them.

"Ran out of gas," M explained. "Thought we'd have enough to get where we're going, but I guessed wrong."

"And what the hell makes you think you could get any gas here?"

"Well it looked like this place maybe had been a gas station, and we thought maybe it still might be one or at least might have some gas left over from when it was."

"Well," said the surly owner, looking toward his fellow card players, "we're just about all out, though we keep on playing, right boys?"

"Just about—" M said, leaping for the last straw.

"Well we might have some small amount of old gas, but the odds are it's all played out—like some people you might know."

"I didn't see any other place around, so I guess, we'd just as soon try what you got as walk out the door with nothing."

"Well you know, it's gonna cost you a pretty penny, we don't give away what we got to sell."

"Right," M said, "I understand," he added, when one of the other two men at the table called out, "Come on, don't take all day, sell him your cutthroat gas and have done with it."

"Can't you see that me and this guy are in the middle of delicate business deal?"

"OK. Ok.," said the card playing friend. "Just get on with it—we can't wait for you all night," he said.

"Well, listen," M said. "I'm willing to pay any reasonable price—"

"Reasonable my ass! You're stuck out here in the middle a nowhere, you walk into the only place around that might have even a drop of gas and you're asking me to set what you think's a reasonable price!"

The third man at the table began to laugh, and M felt the sudden urge to leave, even though it might be miles to go before they found another place that could offer them even a drop of gas.

"Ok," he said, "What's your price? you know you've got me between a rock and a dark place."

"You damn sure straight I do," the owner said. "And how much you think this gas is worth to you?"

"I don't know."

"Well you damn well should know, if you don't have your head up your ass. I guess that it's worth all you got, cause if you don't get it, you might not get any anywhere again and you might end up out of gas for sure, if you can get my drift."

At this point, M saw the situation was almost hopeless. "Look," he said, "I'm traveling light, and I don't have much, so why don't I just give you all I have, and you give me as much gas as you can?"

With that, he pulled out his wallet and opened it, putting the few bills it held on the counter.

"Some forty dollars!" the owner said, spitting out the sum estimated with the greatest contempt. "That's sure a small enough amount for someone who's playing out his last cards," he said. "So I'll tell you what we're gonna do," he continued. "You give me this money and throw in the bike too, and then I'll give you the gas and we'll call it a night."

"Why would I want the gas if I had to give up my bike to get it."

"That's for you to figure out," was the answer. "Sometimes that's just the way things are."

"But—" M stammered at a loss for words.

"But, my ass," said the owner. "You, know, I'm just about sick of your whines and wherefores, just about sick of dealing with you at all, so why don't you just get the fuck out of here, so I can get back to my card game."

M didn't know what to say. He reached for his wallet and tried to put it back in his pocket. And at that point, the owner grabbed his arm and twisted the wallet out of his hand.

"None of this," he said. "You offered the money and now you try to take it back? None of this bullshit."

And with that, M tried to break free, and the owner struck him in the stomach. M tried to fight back, flailing away at the owner. But it was to no avail, none of his blows had any effect.

"Looks like this ole boy's got no bounce to the ounce," said the owner, hitting him again even harder. "Looks like he's all washed up," he said "he's out of cards to play"

And with that. the card players laughed their heads off, as M staggered out of the store, with no money left, with, as he suddenly realized, the girlfriend nowhere to be seen and him with no place or person to turn to.

"But why should I be surprised she's gone and I'm all alone?" he mused. "Who would want to stay with someone who runs out of gas, can't find a way to get any and can't defend himself against those who might have it and decide to keep it?"

Somehow, he managed to get back on his bike, even though he knew it was absurd to do so. And sure enough, the bike sputtered and heaved … but finally, to M's great surprise, suddenly revved up.

"How could this be?" he asked himself. "I was sure I was out of gas, but looks like there something left, even it's maybe just some fumes."

And then M realized he had been running on empty for some time; and on empty, off he went into the night on his way to where and when only God or the Devil might know.

2. M in Flight

I'm on the plane knowing I should write something but feeling tired, so I decide to try writing something simple like the dream I had had the previous night, something I found myself calling "Out of Gas." I guess I might have been pretty much out of gas, because I couldn't get myself to write the story. I tried to read a book and then watch the silly movie they were showing about cars chasing cars, but nothing caught on and I was reduced to looking around to see if there were something or someone that or who could push me toward writing the story.

Just about then, I noticed a young man sitting across the aisle but one seat up ahead, hacking away on a MacBook Air with the greatest of ease and seeming pleasure. I couldn't read a letter he was writing, but it was obvious he was going through a large text, involving lots of lines of dialogue. And I could kind of tell that the writing might be very rich, just by the kind of pleasure and intensity the young man showed as he typed on and on, so rapid, and seemingly carefree, it seemed to me—as if writing were the simplest and most natural thing to do in the world.

Even as I struggled with my own story, I could not help looking over the young man's shoulder to watch him working away. I got lost in my text, couldn't seem to keep the rhythm going which I often needed to rock a story into being. My lead character got distracted and couldn't walk a straight line let alone lend himself to a straight plot. I kept trying to see if I could read what the young man was typing but couldn't make out a phrase or letter. But it was apparent the writing had to be good, because he even laughed at his witty comments sometimes also as he kept on and on. Once in a while, he'd save his material and stop, but even then, his creative juices kept flowing. He put his mac aside, pulled two books out of his bag andO flipped through one, then the other, reading a few pages and marking key passages or phrases. The first seemed to be a novel by Thornton Wilder (an odd, old-fashioned choice, I thought.) The second he clearly made out to Thomas Wolfe's *You Can't Go Home Again* ("that's more the ticket for this prolific young writer," I told myself) regretting that I had not read the book to the end, and knowing that this energetic young writer would do so.

A few back and forth moves between the two books and then he was back to his sleek and so usable computer, flipping it open and again working on a passage of dialogue, seeming to act out each out each word and phrase as he read. Meanwhile I was having trouble with "Out of Gas." The guy in front of me had moved his seat back, making it hard for me to keep my own oversized and plane-impractical laptop functioning. So that I could only open it part way before it hit up against the seat in front of me; and I had to bang out what I could of my story without being able to see the screen. And in the meantime, the young man kept writing out his story, even as I struggled with mine, almost out of gas while writing "Out of Gas."

And then I knew I entirely resented and yes perhaps hated this young man even to the degree I admired him for his agility, energy and commitment to his craft. I knew he was going to work and work, enjoying his work, each event in his life so much raw material for the refinements of his mind and of course others as well. Barring unfortunate accidents (like a plane crash, or, say, a violent act carried out by a rancorous fellow traveler), he would do all the reading and the critical pages of writing to finally reach the point where all his early promise would find its fulfillment. Why couldn't I have been like this young man, so disciplined writing no matter what in life might come to complicate his path and even try to distract him from it? Why had writing become such a painful and unrewarding enterprise that I began to avoid it so many years ago? Why did I have to abandon my writing, giving in to the pains and travails my life brought me, unable to put in all those years of practice that might have enabled me to write better—something truly worthwhile. I'd be spending my early seventies trying to make up for those many years lost, writing with a sense of desperation I could hardly contain, knowing I was starting so damned late, and not knowing if I would ever get any of my pitiful little efforts published by some publisher whose books people might read, let alone if I would write anything sufficiently worth any one's all so limited time to read anything. And all this while, I was watching this young writer writing away, imagining his future books, his great early triumphs, his mid-career crises and then the profound, immortal work that would round out a fine career and life. And all this time I was desperately fearing, as did the character in my story, that I had indeed started too late, and that I was now indeed out of gas.

And now the plane began its descent into San Juan, we were told to put our electronic equipment away, and we both raced to get down our last thoughts on the plane. I writing my final words of "Out of Gas," and he his final corrections, it seemed, of what might well be his first novel. And it was only then that it occurred to me that I really didn't know if he was writing anything at all, but that I'd fantasized the whole thing, but that absurdly all of my jealousy and resentment had indeed egged me on to finish "Out of Gas" in one sitting and indeed develop the raw material for still another story that would accompany and perhaps out-best the first one and certainly anything this callow young man a seat ahead of me and to the right, could possibly have written at his young age, when he was just beginning, so it seemed, to read these all but forgotten W's of U.S. literature, Wilder and Wolfe, when my own career was late in blooming, when I was already old and surely much older than Cervantes when he began his famous book, and I still had hopes to write not *Don Quixote,* but maybe an exemplary novel or story before I was indeed fully and irrevocably out of gas.

3. She on the Same Plane

On the same plane, a few rows back from M, a middle-aged woman was observing him writing away. She also noted how M would look up from his laptop to study a young man sitting one row forward and to the right of him across the aisle who in his turn was writing and reading away almost the entire flight. The woman wore a headphone set and was listening to Brahms' Second Symphony, as she took rapid notes on a pad she always carried with her on her seemingly endless flights and adventures.

Caught up in the sumptuous rhythms and tonalities of Brahms' sweetest masterpiece, she somehow projected the symphony's deepest qualities into her projections with respect to the two males and whatever it might be that they were trying to write. Judging by his movements and shifting positions, she decided that the young man must be writing something terribly erotic and pleasurable—something only a young man or a middle-aged woman could write to the fullest, she decided. As for the older man, he must inevitably be writing out of regret, melancholy and the pain and desperation a man must feel when his powers begin their decline.

She found it strange as, for some reason only she could fathom, she imagined these two would-be writers writing their so different pieces to the same Brahmsian turns, while she, a famed and successful writer who had taken on the most challenging and serious projects always with a sense of purpose and commitment that inevitably led to great success, was on this occasion all but trapped by the commonplace and mediocre fears, frustrations, hopes and disillusions she projected onto these writers to such a degree that her own writing risked falling into mediocrity, only to recover and soar as the Brahms began to reach toward its most sublime moments. And there she was all but victimized but now egged on to triumph by the two would-be writers seated in front of her as the plane, Brahms and her own three-part story reached their greatest heights only to begin the descent or denouement which signaled their end.

Once the plane landed, she quickly scribbled the title to her work, put her pen and pad away, and promptly brought her carry-ons together, moving through the aisle until she passed M and the younger writers as they put their Apples away. "Thank you for your help," she said enigmatically to both, leaving them somewhat confused and distraught as they followed her off the plane and into the concourse where they lost sight of her and of each other as they made their way to their final destinations.

I. Some Life Scenes and Dreams

The Boy Whose Lego Wouldn't Let Go

There once was a boy whose name I can't remember who made Legos whenever he could.

He made tractors and trucks and all kinds of buildings while his brother played the piano and sang karaoke, and who knows what else. And the more his brother played and sang the more he made Legos until the house was filled with more and bigger Legos and his dad had to move his computer to the basement and his mother had to put the new books that came in on the roof.

Then came the day when this boy whose name I probably do remember but don't want to tell you decided he needed to make a Lego who would protect his vehicles and buildings from those who might seek to take them away. He put Lego on Lego until he made a Lego monster so big his head hit the roof, making a big hole and causing momma's books to tumble. Then his feet reached down to the basement smashing the treadmill and the computer and breaking the basement window too.

"Well, my boy," said momma, forced to read her books on the roof, "don't you think you've gone a little too far? "

"Yes, my son," called papa up from the freezing basement, "I think you've gotten out of hand."

As for his brother, he had removed his piano, microphones and speaker to the cold backyard. "I'm tired of playing in the snow," he said, breaking an icicle off his nose.

All three of them were shaking their heads, saying this can't go on. And then he got calls from his grandmas and they said this can't be. But then he got an email from his grandpa saying, here's a gift-card so you can go and buy more Legos. He printed out the card, but the monster Lego snatched it away.

"Let go!" said the boy. But the Lego monster would not let go.

"You've got enough Legos," he told the boy, "I want you to buy me a book and read it to me."

And the little boy who wasn't as little as he'd been last year and whose name I think might have been –oh but I really can't tell after all, looked at his family all covered with snow and looked at his Lego monster just dying to hear a story, and said, "O.k."

And then they were all happy (forever after, some say), and they burst out laughing and shouting, "Happy Birthday."

A Bullied Boy's Birthday Dream

(from "The Little Boy Who Flew Away")

On the night before his birthday, a large ball of snow rolled across the windy field getting bigger and bigger. Linda and Marty ran from it, swiftly rolling a ball of their own. Only theirs was black.

"Hello!" he called, trying to raise his voice above the wind. Linda waved her hand, but Marty kept pushing the ball.

"Come on, Linda!" Marty called.

"But Marty," she answered.

"Marty!" he shouted. Marty pushed the ball aside, took Linda by the hand and stalked off the field. Linda frantically waved as Marty dragged her away. *He will be tall*, he thought as the wind died. *He'll smoke a pipe just like his father*.

"Mmm," a man's voice said.

"Mmm," said Marty's voice.

Marty and his father, dressed the same, sat in identical chairs smoking identical pipes. M, dressed like an orchestra conductor, snapped the stem of a pipe in two.

"Bravo!" thousands cheered, clapping their hands.

M bowed, and Linda begged: "Marry me."

"I'll consider it," he said.

"Please!" she pleaded, kneeling before him. "Please! Please!"

"Rise, Linda," he said with compassion. "I will marry you since you have asked me to do so. You are not perfect. But I will teach you in time."

Water lapped against the ship, wind filled the mast, as they sailed away, she so pretty in her flowing gown, her head upon his shoulder as he steered toward the setting sun. But then when she drew back and smiled, it was not M who, with proud, loving eyes, turned from the helm to her. "Marty!" she cried with joy.

The wind howled. "It's coming! It's coming!" he shouted in panic.

The black ball rolled toward him faster, getting bigger, getting faster, bigger, huge — crashing against the bowling pins!

And now his stomach grew and grew––and grew a mouth that talked to him. "Mm, that was good," said the stomach in a voice that was high-pitched and wheedling, cheerful, yet insistent, all at once. "Mm, yes, I want more."

Thousands of children watched him and laughed as he sat on a stage surrounded by heaps of food, stacks and stacks of meats and pies and cakes. Helplessly he stuffed himself, as the laughter grew louder, and his stomach demanded:

"Yes more. Mm... more. Give me more. I won't ever stop."

"No," said M, stuffing his mouth.

"Eat I say. You wouldn't want to make me die. If I die, you die. So eat. Fill me up. Make me grow."

Trucks roared along the highways blowing their horns; airplanes in formation zoomed by; trains from all points made their way to the stage where he sat.

"Eat, eat," said his stomach over and over again. "More," it said, "more," while the children and now the adults–all the people of the world–clapped their hands in rhythm and chanted, "Look at him go, see him go!"

By truck, by plane, by train the food poured in. Begging hands, brown, black, yellow and white, reached out, but the food went into the stacks and heaps beyond the hungry and angry people. The piles of food grew, and so did his stomach.

"My goodness," said the people. "My goodness, he's gone," they said, their voices fading away.

"Please," he whispered, "Please."

And then the stomach, the people disappeared. Father and Mother hovered over him as he continued to eat.

"Grr," growled Mother.

"Grr," growled Father.

They growled at each other in hatred, then smiled sweetly down on him. "Our boy," they simpered.

Mother's tired face grew older and older. Father grew younger, slimmer. His eyes slanted up, his hair turned red. And on his head, he sprouted two horns. "You wouldn't want us to stop, would you, M? Ha! Ha! Ha!"

And now father's laughter merged with the laughter of the boys and girls, with their rhythmic handclapping and their chanting. "M is fat, M is fat," they chanted.

They formed a circle in his living room, laughing,

chanting and clapping their hands, linking their arms, Linda and Marty now with them, and other, new boys and girls with strangely twisted and blurred faces moving around in a circle that ever grew tighter and smaller. The floor was covered with shattered dishes and toys. The party table was overturned. Sandwiches lay in red pools of punch. And amid the wreckage he sat, crying wildly, licking punch-stained icing off huge pieces of birthday cake. The children sang, laughing louder and circling him, but it was not the usual song:

> *Happy birthday,*
> *Happy happy birthday,*
> *This is your day,*
> *But we have all the fun.*

Their singing and laughter rose to a roar, as they spun faster and faster around him. And in the din, familiar voices blurted out, spurring the laughter on.

"You kids," said Officer Brown.

"You'll fly away," said Fran.

"Men, men!" said Mr. Wolfson.

"Mmm," said Marty's father.

"Mmm," said Marty.

"Grr," said mother.

"Grr," said father.

"If I die, you die," said the stomach.

"No, no... No!" he shouted, sitting up in bed. "It's not

my party. It's a little boy's someplace else. I'm not invited."
But the party was his and he knew it. "All right...all right. It's
going to happen. Well, let it...let it!"

And, moved by the force of dreams, he knew what was
coming and what he had to do.

ark Heaven, Dark Earth

(based on a story told in Georg Büchner's *Woyzek*)

Once there was a poor little boy. He had no mother and he had no father. Because everyone was dead, and there was no one left in the whole world. So he went off looking for somebody, anybody, day and night, night and day. But there was no one on the whole black earth. "There's nothing here," he said. "So I'm going to get myself to heaven."

The moon shone out at him like an old friend, like someone he knew. But when he got up to it, it was just a piece a rotten wood. So then he went up to the sun, but when he got up close to it, it was just a dried-up sunflower. So he went up to the stars, but they were just some tiny bits of gold stuck up in the sky as if they were caught in a spider web, but nothing was holding the web up. So he said, "I think I'll be going back home."

But when he got back down to earth, it was just a big upside-down pot. And he was all alone. There was no one home. And So he just sat down and cried for years and years. And part of him is still sitting right there, all lonely and alone, all by himself. But another part roams the earth seeking earthly things, hoping to find some light in it all.

II. Some Life Scenes and Dreams

How High the Moon

"Well, M, what's it gonna be?" Aldo Parks started, "Are we gonna be the husbands of wives who are friends or are we going to be friends on our own?"

Aldo was an alto-saxophonist who taught music classes during the day and played jazz at night. When M's wife Marlena began a friendship with Aldo's wife Eunice, she announced she'd invited them for dinner. The two women worked and chatted away in the kitchen while Aldo and M were drinking bourbon in the living room. That's when Aldo asked his question.

M was taken aback. His approach to these things was generally to see what might happen. "Look, Aldo, we just met a few minutes ago, let's see how things will play out. But of course, let's try."

"To friendship," Aldo toasted,

"Yes," M said, clinking glasses.

M didn't know what friendship with Aldo entailed. The first line of connection had to be jazz, because while he played no instrument, M as no more than a high school kid had seen Miles, Mingus, Monk, Blakey, Coltrane, Rollins and Roach all in their prime in New York, sometimes several nights a week. His rebel Jewish sensibility had fed on hard bop, and he knew all the ins and outs of the post-Charlie Parker jazz renaissance in Manhattan. Aldo could relate to this and they could talk for hours about the newest jazz innovations, and on this basis, they began developing a friendship, pairing with their wives at concerts, movies and the like, often going to hear Aldo play at the few different venues San Diego had to offer.

Extremely good-looking, with gleam in eyes and smile, Aldo was undoubtedly a competent group player. He never played a wrong note and was always an asset, but he never seemed to take off on his solos. M was disturbed about Aldo's lack of musical fire. It wasn't that all he did was bland and conventional. Aldo was a hard-bopper to be sure. But he flirted with but just couldn't get past his limits. You'd be sitting there waiting him to take off on a flight to somewhere, but the plane stayed on the runway. It was worse than listening to a listless player. His look, the tone of his horn and his cool jazz demeanor made you think that great music would be coming. Sometimes it would even seem to be happening; but then, as if he'd gone further than he could sustain, he'd retreat into the inevitable riffs and musical quotes of the post-Parker era.

This, M reflected, had to tell him something about the man as well as the musician. He'd been born and raised in Philadelphia by a tough-minded washerwoman mother who insisted he take up an instrument and do well in school, but she taught him never to let the music get the better of him, to pursue his teaching credential so he'd have a steady job and square meals for him and his family. Serving in the military, he was stationed in Panama, playing in the military band and sitting in at nightclubs, where he'd met Eunice. And now they'd come to San Diego where he'd secured his first regular teaching job and she entered the School of Social Work, where she'd met up with Marlena. The couple looked just great, he dark black, slim and Sidney Portier-handsome, she light-skinned *mulata*, slim and sexy with a speaking voice that purred half way between Eartha Kitt and Nina Simone. But Aldo seemed too careful a guy who would never get carried away, never go beyond certain limits of decency and decorum. So even though it was he who proposed and pushed for their establishing a friendship, that relationship, for all its good moments never got too far or deep.

No better indication of the limits involved in their possible friendship manifested itself when, much to his dismay, M realized that the whole couple dating routine was a sham, that the two women had become lovers, and were just fronting the couple business so they could socialize together as much as possible. And when he also realized that in a matter of weeks, the women turned extreme, setting forth like hunters, sometimes co-seducing and co-bedding other women as their experiments seemed to turn into a kind of madness that spread like a forest fire burning everything in its path.

Realizing this, M began to feel a sense of excitement. Either he too would share sexual adventures with his wife, or their untenable marriage would come to an end. And if that happened, then he might experience the freedom her ruthless ways made him think he was prepared for, as he went forward on his own. On the other hand, what most disturbed him was his sense that Aldo didn't maybe know what was going on, and then even worse, his inability to treat Aldo like a friend and tell him what was happening. In fact, he felt guilty thinking that if he had been a real friend to Aldo, he'd have warned him right off of Marlena's sexual orientation and her need for conquest. But he had done nothing; and now that the worst was happening, he felt so lost as to what he should do that a silence began to permeate the relationship. A secret had raised its head; and, once having started, and days turning into weeks and months, it was even harder to switch back and reveal the truth when, it would become clear, he had been harboring and not showing this truth as any loyal friend would.

Soon the worst happened, as Marlena traveled to Ensenada with him and insisted they go to a strip show, where she was overwhelmed by a fit of passion for one of the girls and asked M buy her some flowers. She apparently wanted the woman, but when M suggested they share her, she begged off, cursing his raw male sexuality and her inability to fulfill her fantasies with him around. The chance to do something slipped away as the stripper left the club. He and his frustrated wife made it back to their empty hotel room, and he tried to coax her by kissing and touching and then fully making love to her, all the while narrating a fantasy intercourse with the stripper. But try as she might, she couldn't reach orgasm and turned from him, thanking for his efforts but explaining that, as she put it in her brutal honesty, something got in the way.

Some days later, Marlena disappeared with Eunice and M realized they had taken off for Ensenada. Maybe she wished to share with Eunice the fantasy she felt M had foiled. Whatever, it was, this unannounced takeoff was about the last straw. But as his marriage came crashing to its end, M made no effort to have contact with Aldo, no attempt to see or even call him. Soon his marriage was indeed over, the papers signed, and Marlena left the San Diego area, presumably leaving Eunice behind and, so he heard, also in the process of divorce. M cleaned up his house and invited a friend to move in with him. Then, after all the dust had settled, he decided it was time to deal with what he'd felt unable to deal with before.

So it was that he made it to a club where Aldo was playing. And there he was, as handsome as ever, with a cadre of friends, cheering him on as he played his mediocre solos that never went too far.

After the set, he came over to M's table. "Thought that was you," he said. "How's life treatin' you?" he asked.

"Still getting over it," **M** said. "But I'm pretty sure it's all for the best."

"You can bet your bottom dollar on it," said Aldo. "I broke up with Eunice almost the same time you broke up."

"Sorry I didn't call you," M said.

"Yeah, I'm sorry I didn't call you, because I felt pretty guilty about not warning

you about Eunice from the beginning."

M stared at him in surprise. "You mean you knew?"

"Yeah, she was always the seducer of men and women. I should've let you know."

"And I guess I should've let you know, because it was the same with Marlena." "Well, now we both know."

"Yeah," he said, "But it doesn't say much for the friendship we talked about..."

"Well I guess we made some big mistakes."

"Well, let's get better," M said. "Because, now we're free."

The break ended, and Aldo joined the other musicians on stage. And somehow it was a revelation, for never had Aldo played better. His horn rose and soared, his invention was consummate, remarkable. In one chorus he evoked the Bird, in another it was Sonny Stitt, and then Sonny Rollins, and then Adderley and Eric Dolphy. He played out repetitions and variations of rhythmic and melodic patterns, interspersed with staccato and semi-detached trills, interrupted by sudden flourishes and swoops. His runs roared, with jarring passages and furious double-time spurts. He seemed to be shouting and gesticulating on his horn, as if he were waving his audience into battle and heading toward some tumultuous victory over race and tribulation, love and betrayal—over any and everything. On he went gliding, taking flight, reaching deep down, only to rise again, spreading out with one chorus leading to another and another, each one with variation on variation until it was Coltrane all Coltrane, and then Bird mixing with Coltrane and all the others, until it was finally Lonnie Parks who came forward standing tall and brave and now reaching out and taking off the earth as he soared, letting loose and flying high and then higher—higher even than the moon.

The Cabbage Soup: A Double Header

1.

With M's career in the shade, his mother came on her annual visit to the family in Minnesota, where his second wife Elena had a teaching slot with a future, while he, with a Ph.D. like her, and now age thirty seven, had failed to get an academic position and was working as a migrant worker counselor in St. Paul. One day, M announced that his friends, Bob and Dina along with Dina's two kids, Luis and Daniel, would be coming to dinner that evening, and he asked his mother if she would do the honors of making her famous cabbage soup for the occasion.

M's mother would sit at home waiting for her son to return from work while she was left alone wondering why she had even bothered to visit a house whose occupants had so little time to spend with her. Even David, Elena's son M had adopted, seemed to have little time for her, although he always tried to be polite and friendly. But despite it all, she stubbornly came for her visits, and M always attended her as best he could in the evenings and weekends when he was free. So, would Elena, though she was constantly busy at the university or, in this case, preparing a paper for a conference which would leave M and visiting mother to their own devices for much of the time during her stay.

But now, to have a specific request from her son to do something that she was truly gifted at doing, to prepare her own magnificent version of one of the key foods of M's childhood and to do so not only for him but also his family and his friends and sons, was for her a fine chance for an activity that honored her abilities and at least somehow redeemed an otherwise eventless, empty and in many ways depressing visit.

So, on the designated evening for the special dinner treat, when M and Elena returned from their jobs, they found his mother's soup simmering on the stove. M quickly sliced the two rye breads he'd bought to accompany the soup, while his wife put the finishing touches on a simple dessert, now made more complex and rich with the addition of the sweet cream and some almonds. When the guests finally arrived, all was ready, and they sat down to their bowls of soup and seconds as Bob wondered at a soup so like the wonderful one he remembered his own mother making, and Dina purred with what she claimed was the greatest soup in creation, and one she was so happy her sons could also enjoy.

"It was this soup and not the apple by which the serpent tempted Eve and she Adam until they were dismissed from Paradise, she condemned to the labor pains of birthing and he the pains of earning the bread of every day," M announced, as he buttered a second batch of rye slices, so that with the soup, the group would at least earn the fruit and booty of their labors. And meanwhile M's mother cooed as she heard the oohs and ahs watching her adopted grandson and Dina's two sons who were his friends, as they sipped and slurped their way through one serving of soup and bread after another.

"My mother taught me to make this soup before she died when I was still a little girl," she said.

"It's the best version of Eastern European borsht I know," said M, playing the part of Jewish gourmet. "With just the right touch of sugar, tomato, beef (what we call *flunken*) and that special touch of sour salt, without any cream (that wouldn't be kosher) or anything that might make it more Russian, Polish or Romanian than truly Jewish."

The adults laughed at the overly detailed explanation, and M's mother shouted, "Enough explanation, my son the atheist and Ph.D. doctor of Yiddish foods who can't get a teaching job!" she finished, almost crying and looked over at Elena with an accusing eye, as if somehow, she could have gotten her boy at least got something like the fine job she had.

"I'm sorry, but I can't help what I feel," she said, as a hush fell over the group with this load of motherly guilt, suffering and recrimination. But this awkward moment turned from tension to mirth, as all adult heads turned again to the young boys, who filled a fourth plate, and then a fifth, slurping away, spilling soup on napkin, table cloth and wherever, before reaching the last point of no return at which the adults had arrived some time before.

"Mom, that was a great soup," M said when the guests finally left.

"They all seemed to like it," she said.

"Though maybe you made it too sour and not sweet enough this time," said Elena.

2.

On another of the annual visits to Minnesota by his mother, M asked her to make a second batch of her wonderful soup—this time to treat and honor Tom, a friend he and Elena had especially treasured for some time, and who would be arriving with her from a week-long upstate summer conference they were both attending. M's mother agreed, hoping not only to satisfy her son's wish, but also to provide him a token reminder of her love even after she had left town or even the world. However, her plans were to be as frustrated as were her dreams for her son.

Days of her visit went by with her preparing her cabbage soup even while she watched her TV favorites and knitted slippers for every member of her family and friends, while M went off each day to counsel and help migrant farmworkers, and Elena went off to the conference which she told them would help determine the future of the field in which she and Tom both worked. The conference over, and now all revved up with new visions of what was to be done, Elena came back to Minneapolis with Tom.

And then it came to pass—as Tom sat down to participate in the banquet arranged in his honor, in which he was able to savor a significant if modest portion of M's mother's miraculous soup. As those assembled gave *testimonio* to this sweet and sour wonder, the visiting professor, a brilliant young Marxist, could not resist commenting on the soup's subversive danger. "Maybe we shouldn't eat so much of this elixir," he suggested. "It's enough to distract and seduce vulnerable radical scholars from the primary contradictions of Capital," he quipped.

That night, perhaps inspired by a soupy dream, and unable to sleep further, Tom rose from his bed to explore whatever leftovers there might be in the refrigerator. After quietly, ever so quietly, opening several packages, he came upon the jar of the brew for which he so longed, emptied the jar and promptly heated its contents.

The very next morning, M's mother, the first to rise, made her way to the kitchen to prepare a small farewell breakfast for the visiting friend; and there, upon the briefest investigation, she found the package that had held that jar that should have contained M's soup and now contained—nothing. M's mother, knocked on the bedroom door.

"M!" She whispered hoarsely. M quickly met her in the hallway.

"What's going on mom?"

"I just looked at the cabbage soup jar, and it's all gone. Did you eat it?"

"No, mom," M answered, hardly able to keep his eyes open.

"Well then, who did? Who stole your soup?"

"Tom probably ate it, mom, no big deal."

"No big deal!" she all but shouted, scandalized. "I worked and worked on your soup, and out of love for you I even give him some, and now he just goes and eats all the rest that I prepared just for my son."

"Mom," M chided, trying to calm her.

"Don't mom me," she said, probably angrier than he had ever seen her, "I serve you all a dinner fit for a King, and this is how he rewards you, blaming your problems on my soup and then eating up all I had especially prepared for you."

"Mother," M said." "You can't go on like this really— Tom naturally thinks a refrigerator at a friend's house is his to open—he's a socialist, mom! And he thinks that a soup made by a friend's mother is his soup too. You have to realize too, Mom, that Tom's always trying to help me with my crazy career, no matter what little joke he might make at dinner, So I don't want to hear another word about this." He all but menaced her. "He's going today, and I want him to go in peace, without your saying anything angry or snide or anything. I don't want you to say a word about the soup or criticize him in any way, you understand? Because despite what you might think he is my friend—and one of the best friends I'm lucky enough to have."

"What kind of friend would eat the soup a mother's made his friend's son?" she insisted.

"Enough! The soup was made for him, and he ate more of it than you wanted him to—that's all!"

And for sure, M's mother behaved, and Tom took his plane to home without further incident, and without ever knowing of the distress and rage he had provoked.

Some years later, his marriage long a thing of the past, M finally won an academic job, and was now launched on a new project that would probably mean tenure. Eager to give cheer to his aging mother, finally glowing with the new fortune of a son who was very belatedly making her proud, he called to tell her the good news.

"So, a real book it is, this time, one all by you?"

"Well yes, it's a real book," M said, "not another edited volume, but one I'm co-writing for a major university press.

"And who's the co-author," she asked, as astute and suspicious as ever.

"You remember him, mom," M found himself saying, but getting ready to hold his breath.

"Not the one who ate your cabbage soup!" she exclaimed.

"Yes mom, the one who always finds value in what I do."

"Value!" she barked. "A man who eats the soup a mother's made for her son! "

"Ay, mom," said M. "Gotta go! Talk to you later."

"M, mark my words," she warned, "he'll eat all the soup all over again!"

And it was she, not he, who hung up the phone.

The Parking Space

One warm spring day, M drove down to his psychologist's office in the medical center on Columbus Drive in hopes of finding a parking space in time for his post-divorce therapy session as he sought to recover from his second marriage. To be sure, he was not late, but he had been intent in arriving early to find one of the few metered parking places that would enable him to avoid the stiff parking fee in the city garage. As he passed the center entrance and made his way north along the drive, he spotted a car pulling out up ahead. M sped up to take advantage of the new opening, when to his surprise and chagrin, a man in a pickup truck going in the opposite direction made an illegal u-turn and nosed his way into the spot toward which M had been driving.

Outraged against the enormous injustice of the act he had just seen perpetrated against him, enraged by the injustice of a universe in which the cops were never around when you needed them. M could not merely drive on, but felt impelled and compelled to pull up alongside the criminal pickup driver, unroll the passenger side window and directing himself toward the face behind the driver's unrolled window, initiate the classic confrontation between urban Jew and country bumpkin pickup driving redneck, with all the dimensions of ethnic and class struggle one could impute to such an encounter.

"You know what you did was illegal, right?" he began, evoking the laws of Moses—or was it Hammurabi? "You know you broke the law to take my spot."

"Well," said the driver, already flummoxed, "I don't care. I saw the spot and I took it and now it's mine—you'd have done the same thing if you were me."

"Don't be so sure," M said. "Some of us don't do things like that."

"Well I did it, and now I'm here," the truck-driver insisted.

"Look," said M, fed up with all the small talk. "Someday not too long from now you're going to get old and sick, and you'll be miserable and all alone and you're going to wonder what you did to deserve your terrible fate of suffering and dying in agony. And at that moment, you're going to suddenly remember this very day and minute and the way you robbed me of this parking spot, and you'll understand, but it'll be too late, there'll be nothing you can do about it."

And with that M drove off looking for another spot.

In fact, it was not easy to find one, but since he was still relatively early, M continued seeking an alternative to the high-priced lot. On around and around he went, probably wasting more in gas that he would have in paying for a parking lot. But having no luck, he all but gave up and made his way again past the medical center with only a last glimmer of hope that he might find a metered spot before he reluctantly accepted his fate and entered the high-priced parking venue. And lo and behold, he saw himself approaching the metered spot of his recent encounter; and there indeed was the pickup truck, and now M could see a flashing a left turn signal light, and, yes, an arm-waving toward him as the vehicle moved off, leaving M the space he had so deeply coveted.

M could not but be impressed, but at the same time appalled by what had happened. As he properly backed into the parking space, he looked up ahead toward the pickup truck, where the driver was now extending his fist in the air, signaling the victory of Right. M looked at the truck and thought of the driver.

"Poor schmuck," he heard himself say with genuine compassion and much condescension, ready now to explore his psychological problems with at least this small victory to buoy up his spirits.

The Cake

It was M's misfortune to be entirely vulnerable to food and to have as his only study space a room adjacent to the kitchen which as in every Latino household served as the center for conversation as well as eating. Of course, the usual action in the kitchen had to do with coffee drinking or the engorging of mountains of rice and beans, with chicken, codfish and, often enough, pork. But one day M, overweight and on one of his countless diets that always went so well until sidetracked by one thing or another, had the misfortune of misfortunes to have the flow of his writing turned off as he witnessed his third wife and her daughter come home with a chocolate cake and begin eating it ever so slowly while they conversed about this relative or that in their endlessly extended family.

M was in the throes of one of his many troubled attempts to write a story, when he was overwhelmed by the smell of chocolate mixed with mocha and cherry, and his imaginary drifted from its oh-so-important literary concentration to the sheer thrill of savoring the cake's sweet and delicious richness. Indeed, it was an exquisite and delicate cake; and mother and daughter were treating on what he could sense were tiny slices with the greatest daintiness imaginable. On and on they talked, only ever so often breaking the smallest possible piece from the cake, savoring it slowly in their mouths until they finally finished off their portions and, apparently without even thinking about it, placed the tasty remains of the cake in its original package, closed the box and placed it in the refrigerator.

His wife then said, "M, we're off. Good luck with your story,"

"O.k.," he said, "have a good time."

And then the two women left the house, leaving M to his fictional efforts and an imagination focused entirely not on the work at hand but on the piece of work sitting in its box inside the refrigerator.

M sought to forget the cake, but the women would not return for some time; and hard as he might, he found his brain returning to the cake time and time again. Why after all should he not have the smallest piece of that delicious treat? Did not the sweat of his brow at least contribute however indirectly to its purchase? And what did it matter if he had the smallest portion, because after all it would hardly be noticed. At least he should be entitled to take a tiny taste if only to see what he was missing, especially since he had suffered so much temptation and torture. And with these justifications clearly enunciated, he felt no compunction about taking the smallest sliver from the cake. Once decided, he acted decisively and took out the cake box, opened it and took that ever so infinitesimal slice, and then scooping a small portion of that minute slice onto his awaiting fork and bringing it to and then into his awaiting mouth.

The divine taste of the cake flooded his mouth and it dawned upon him that in Eden the forbidden fruit must have been covered with chocolate... His tongue swirled the chocolate about until it reached every taste bud; he savored the flavor with half parted eyes and growing fervor, taking a second bite which all but finished off the tiny slice and left him now in the throes of an ecstatic pleasure. Only a few, chocolate crumbs remained, and these he scooped onto his fork with the knife, and quickly devoured, as if heaping some added fuel onto an already peaking flame.

Then, waiting just a few seconds, listening to hear if any sound in the house might indicate the return of the women or someone who could infringe his privacy and witness his violation of the laws governing his dietary restrictions. Then he closed the cake box and returned it to the place it had been in the refrigerator, cleaning the table, the knife and fork, and putting these telltale implements in the dishwasher, made his way back to his study and his important work at hand.

On he worked word processing away, but within minutes he found himself losing concentration as his mind focused ever more on the cake in the box in the fridge in the kitchen next to the room where he worked. He brushed it aside and clicked away, but then he could resist it no more. The flavors of the cake, the chocolate, the aftertaste of cherry and mocha overcame him, till he finally went to the refrigerator, opened the door and stared at the cake box, eventually taking it out, opening it and examining the cake. No damage done so far, nothing noticeable, and he estimated he could take even a bit more without detection. This decided, he went for the knife and attempted the smallest possible incision again into the cake. But just at the decisive moment, his hand slipped just a big, and M found that he had left a gash which would not be easy to hide no matter what he might do. At this crucial moment, he reacted in a kind of outrage. After all, how unfair they were to buy this temptation, to keep it within his reach and eat only the smallest piece from it. Was he not an economic force in the house? Did he have no rights here? What were his marriage and relations about anyway? And so, in this state of self-defense and justification, M decided that he did indeed have a story of his long but frustrated career as a writer. These perspectives now firmly entrenched, he made an even broader slice into the cake, and severed his piece from the rest, putting that bit on his plate and then having a go at it with gusto.

This done, his rights staked out, M again put the cake back into the box, closed the lid and placed it back on the shelf. He rinsed the knife, fork and plate and putting them away before returning to his little room off the kitchen, where now well-served and contented he felt he would have all the more energy to write the most wonderful text that he had in him to write.

But then, once again, before he could get fully carried away with his now cake-inspired and cake-fueled creative process, he felt himself enveloped with an overwhelming desire to partake more fully of the cake with which he now viewed as the symbolic battlefield of his marriage, his creativity and very being. But on this third round, with his invasion now visible,

M showed no quarter nor took any prisoners. It was after all too late to cover his tracks, no way to deny violation of diet and trust, so why bother at all? Why not just live out one's passion wherever it took him? Why not go all out in the face of all the objections and recriminations? What did life mean if one were trapped and had to give up all one loved or felt compelled to need?

So this time he could hold back no more, this time he risked digging deep into the cake, lacerating and practically devouring it, driven almost wild by the smell of chocolate with mocha and cherry, eating away without restraint until there was nothing left of it, until it was completely gone. Then, crazed and sated, he sat staring at what he had done, quick to pick up any remaining crumbs and eating them too, and then placing the now empty cake plate into the cake box, staring at the box, and wondering what if anything he could do.

What would he say when his wife returned? What could he do but grim smugly grin and tell her, "Someone came in and stole it," or "A bear devoured it," or "The cat did it in—end of story." But these would lead to horrendous dénouements, horrible ways to bring things to a conclusion. What did they say about him and all his creativity? He was a bust, he knew **all** it, all this pretense of writing was for naught. Clearly, he was a failure, a slave to his compulsions and needs, no better than a crackhead or any junkie. And now he would be revealed, his lack of will and imagination exposed, that cat out of the bag at last.

But surely there had to be some way better than all this. Surely there had to be a way that would at least create the illusion of success, despite all the weakness involved. He was after all a writer, and one of his tricks was to lay out difficult situations and then find his way out of them. He remembered an early story where he'd found such a solution, and when he showed the story to a friend who indeed knew about writing, and the friend told him he had talent and that he should indeed develop it. And here he was trying again almost forty years later, without having written more than a story a decade in all those years, but with his obesity growing virtually in inverse relation to his lack of production. Now was his chance to modify that relationship, even though he would be breaking the rules and his pact with the devil, even though he knew it could only speed on his eventual and inevitable end.

Returning to his writing desk, the cake box still sitting like defiant evidence on the kitchen table, he sat down and tried to reason out all that had happened until he came to the part where he sat down at the table to write; and in that moment, with the words of his friend some forty years before still ringing in his ears, it became all too clear to him what he had to do. So he wrote it down—how the author suddenly went to the kitchen garbage pail and opened it to find the bag in which the cakebox had been placed, and sure enough there on the bag was the name and address of the bakery where his wife and her daughter had bought the cake. And so he continued to write how he took out the bag and stuffed the cake box in it, went down the back stairs and dumped it all in the garbage outside. Then he got in his car and headed off to the bakery where indeed he found the same cake, purchased it and brought it home, almost flying on his pudgy legs up the stairs and through the back door leading to the kitchen, where he proceeded to open the cake box, and cut out a little more than the equivalence of two slim slices from it, and sat down to eat them with the greatest of delicacy and pleasure until, having left the cake looking almost but not quite as it had when the women had left, he returned the cake to the box, put the box in the fridge and then put the bag in the garbage pail.

When the women returned home sometime later, there he was at his desk writing about their return. And just as he was narrating it, his wife looked at him and said, "Why do you have some chocolate on your chin?"

"Because I couldn't resist that cake, I just had to have a sliver of it," he answered.

"Well I guess a little bit's not so bad," she said. "And your story?"

"Just finishing it up."

"And how is it?"

"A piece of cake," he said.

How the Argentines Learned to Dance Salsa

So now, after so many years, M, accompanied by his third wife, was finally in one of his dream cities, Buenos Aires, in the winter, but Buenos Aires nevertheless. And what a beautiful city it was, with all the delights he'd been waiting so long to see, now just a cab ride away. Of course, he had to look for writers and academic friends, as well as countless bookstores; and that would complicate his stay. But surely, whether he fulfilled his scholarly agenda or not, he could have a grand time just by eating the *parilladas*, *empanadas* and pizzas, drinking the trapiche and above all seeking out tango performers—to watch the dancers and above all see and hear the singers and above all else the musicians who made tango such a delight.

Things began well enough at the art museum, though most of the wonderful Latin American and Argentine collection was out on tour. Then he found a small museum featuring a show on "The Times of Gardel." The show was so fine, with its tango posters, film clips and period paraphernalia, with the great *tanguero* singing "Por una cabeza" and other fine songs. And in the museum lobby, he was able to purchase the tickets for the best tango club in town, plus discounted tickets to see *Rigoletto* at the Teatro Colón.

Still when they got back to their hotel room, M's wife called his attention to a newspaper headline from *La Nación* that had immediately caught her rapt attention. Look, she said. *Puerto Rico vence, y los Yanquis* go home! And sure enough, M read on to discover that the Puerto Rican basketball team had won a major game against the U.S. team in the World Cup of Basketball.

"And tonight, they're going to play the USSR," she told him, adding that maybe they could still get tickets.

"But we're in Buenos Aires," he said, "and we've tickets for tango."

"But this is the Puerto Rican team—the coach is from my hometown," she reported and then added, "That tango club is there every night but there's only one night when a Puerto Rican team plays the USSR after beating the U.S."

Her logic was impeccable. With one phone call he was able to cancel out his tango tickets, and then they both walked several blocks to the ticket office at Luna Park, where they were able to purchase their seats. That night, they watched as the Puerto Rican team shined but eventually faded before the fierce, aggressive onslaught of Soviet forces. Still, there were lots of Puerto Rican fans who had come to the Games and proudly waved their flags, pushing the entire Argentine public to join them in applauding the Puerto Rican team for their gallant victory over their colonial masters and their fine showing against the country that was their master's greatest foe.

After the game, M suggested they should try to go to dinner and a show in La Boca, that section of the city so marked by its Italian working classing immigrant ambiance, that it had been dubbed "La República de la Boca." "That's like saying "La República de Puerto Rico," his wife said, agreeing to go. The fact was that La Boca was also a tourist trap where foreigners gathered for large plates of pasta and a show that frequently paid tribute to the visiting guests. Sure enough, after the wine, the pasta and yes, the beef, the house band musicians took their places on stage, and played an opening tango; and then an emcee stepped forward and welcomed the visiting public, first by making a few semi-obscene jokes and then asking people where they came from.

"From Santa Fe," said one young man.

"From Cordoba!" shouted another, as the audience applauded.

"Montevideo," a woman called out;

"Sao Paulo!" called out another, and the crowd roared.

And then, somehow, it was his wife's turn. "Puerto Rico!" she shrieked at the top of her lungs.

And with that the crowd exploded. "Viva Puerto Rico!" they intoned clapping and whistling, flushed with the Boricua team's showing in the games.

"*Yanqui* go home!" shouted someone in the crowd, and the people applauded again. And now after a few whispers from the emcee to their leader, the band began playing not another tango, but the best they could do with a salsa.

M was not a dancer, and his wife hated dancing with him. But still when the music began to play, he surveyed the audience quickly and noted that, aside from a few couples, the public mainly consisted of pairs of men on the prowl and an entire football team from Rosario. He knew what could happen in these circumstances, that someone was going to ask Amelia to dance and once the pattern was set, one after another would come forward, while he'd be sitting like an idiot, trying to smile as all these machistic bastards would seek to take liberties, with his wife enjoying the whole thing. It was time to act, and act he did.

"Mira, Amelia," he said. "I know you don't like to dance with me, but you're going to get up and dance with me right now."

With that he rose, and she only murmured "okay," as he drew her out of her chair and onto the dance floor, while the crowd broke into raucous cheers. On and on they applauded as M and his wife took their spin, and gradually as other couples joined the fray.

On and on the couple danced, though M struggled to make the simplest turns, stumbling or tripping at each crucial moment. As the dancing continued, he looked toward the other couples and saw that many were doing odd gyrations and even stranger turns and passes, moving their shoulders rather than their hips, and looking somewhat like a bunch of monkeys playing Simple Simon Says.

"Why are they dancing so weird?" He asked his wife, giving her another twirl.

"*Porque te están imitando,*" she said. "They're imitating you."

And So the pattern was set as one couple taught another in la Boca, across the city and throughout the country. So that it was M, indeed it could be said, who failed to see a tango program, let alone learn how to dance the dance, but who on one special occasion, taught the Argentine people how to dance salsa.

"And," M mused, "it may well be that this is the pattern of all I've done with Latin America and my life."

*I*n Paris and Venice: Three Wives
in a Race-Tinged Triptych

1.

One crisp October day, during his first stay in Paris, M, age 24, walked briskly with his first wife down the Boulevard San Michel in the Left Bank's Latin Quarter and saw coming toward them an African or Afro-Caribbean man shouting indecipherable words coupled with defiant gestures suggesting such a state of agitation and anger that M immediately feared that they or at least he might become the immediate object of some unpredictable and overheated form of violence stemming from who knew what source of outrage or abuse. On the other hand, he did not wish to submit to any appearance of racial bias or fear. These conflicting impulses led him to neither turn away nor desist in his walk even as the man grew closer to him. M moved forward, firmly urging his wife along with him, though to one side of the anticipated crossing point of the two men. As they came upon each other, M maintained a thin, timidly friendly smile on his face, which the African or African Caribbean man greeted with a punch which landed flush like a shock of lightning on our hero 's nose. The man continued his walk as M fell to the cold sidewalk only to bounce up again, lean against his wife and use his gloved[?] hand to stop the excessive flow of blood issuing from his nose.

54

"Well," said his wife. "So much for your liberal Jewish politics and so much for our first time in Paris.

2.

Years later, M, age 35, is in a metro station late one night with his second wife and son, when another man, apparently drunk, approaches and asks for a handout. M tells him no, unwilling to contribute to his apparent addiction.

The man eyes M up and down. "*Juif,*" he mutters.

"Are you talking to me?" M asks imitating de Niro, but in his own funky French. "You know what you are," he sputters.

"Tell him I can kick the shit out of his goy ass," he tells his wife, asking her to translate, which she refuses to do, pulling him on to the train which has just arrived.

"*Juif! Salou!*" M can see him mouthing through the door, as the train pulls out.

M gives him the finger and his new friend kicks against the closed train door.

3. Shylock Shy Luck
(A Variant Based on "Menace in Venice")

M, now 72, is with his third wife, Puerto Rican and rather feisty, in a Venice hotel, where they are having a frustrating time with the manager, who turns literary on them. "It is said that Venice is a labyrinth of problems," the manager observes—"a comedy of errors, a place of masks and dangers, resentments, disguises and paybacks big and small… Have you read the story by your wonderful Edgar Allen Poe?"

"Who has not?" M answers. "But have you read *Morte a Venezia*?" he asks. "Ha! I see you are an educated man. But remember above all your beloved Shakespeare."

"I do," M assures him.

"In this case, if I may say so, you are Shylock, even though you think it is I who demands the pound of flesh."

M's is torn between amusement and outrage at the literary game and of course the racial profiling.

To make matters worse, the manager realizes that M's wife is from the Caribbean. "No, no—no trouble, be happy," he says, "to quote a song of yours," he tells her, seeming not to notice how offended M knows her to be. "Don't worry—not to worry at all," he said, "You'll be happy in our little hotel."

Later that day, they wander out along the waterways trying to decide what to do during their short stay. M, at last, seeing a sign advertising a past performance of Rickie Martin, takes a shot of Amelia in front of the poster, buys them tickets for a play not by Shakespeare but by Goldoni, and then says, "Let's visit the Jewish quarter."

They follow their guidebook instructions, taking a *vaporetto* and then asking people along their way until they finally find themselves in Europe's oldest ghetto. Soon they are touring synagogues with a guide who describes the Sephardic community, and then the coming of the Ashkenazi with the booming Adriatic economy—of how the Doggi protected them but held them in check by their ghettoization. Going into one place and another, M is struck by the different plaques commemorating the deceased. It seems that all the wildly different names of the Jewish diaspora Italian-style are spread out before him; and among them are the many Levis who remind him of Carlo and Primo, two of Italy's most famous authors, the second being one of the most telling writers of the Holocaust. At which point, M recalls Primo's account of the rounding up of the Italian Jews, and their transport to Auschwitz.

His image of the country turns terribly grim and he seeks to express his sense of ethnic solidarity by lunching at the famed restaurant on the main business street of the ghetto. There he and Amelia have a combination plate featuring Ashkenazi as well as Sephardic seeming dishes, while he speaks to her of the slaughter of his fellow tribe members.

That evening even as they watch Goldoni's *A Servant of Two Masters*, M, seeing the Commedia dell'arte inflections of the production, has the most profound sense that he and Amelia themselves are part of a *commedia* as harlequinesque buffoons continually slipping on Caribbean banana peels on some slippery canal-drenched street.

When the couple returns to the hotel, M tells the manager about their trouble using their television. The Manager goes to their room, resets the TV system but then mocks them. "You are *Americani*, you should know technology, no?"

"I'm from Puerto Rico," Amelia reminded, as her resentment rose.

"Ah, but you belong to the *Americani!*" he says smugly apparently proud to show off his knowledge.

"No more than we belong to you," Amelia retorts.

"Of course, as you wish, you are guests after all," the manager says, retreating from the room.

"Well, at least we have television, "M says, but when he tries to change the channel, the set goes dead again. He tries to adjust it but again to no avail. He then tries to call the manager back but cannot not get through to the front desk. He then starts to put on his pants to go downstairs. But Amelia stops him.

"Forget about it," she said, "it's useless trying to talk to an asshole," and she fell off to sleep.

M reads a bit and considers Shakespeare's racism and anti-Semitism, Goldoni's view of Venice and the nasty hotel manager's take on everything. M realizes that he and Amelia are virtually two servants of one Venetian master. And then he too falls asleep.

Return to Bellagio

1.

And so it was that M and Amelia were once again in Como, looking out of the blue lake as they ate their cheese, bread and olives and sipped their wine, watched the wind-kissed sailboats streaming toward one island or another as the couple tried to decide which routes they might explore on their way to Stresa on Lago Maggiore. All this time he had thought they would scoot up the road to visit Bellagio ever so briefly before returning to take the route and ferry that would lead them to their next hotel. But now, Amelia looked at the map and had her doubts. "I don't know," she said, "it's out of our way and we've been there before. What's new to see? Why should we waste the gas and energy?"

" Because I want to write another Italian story," he said, "And it's about returning to Bellagio."

"But do you have to return to Bellagio to write about returning there? Why can't you just write it?"

"Because that's against the rules," he explained. "The trick is not to make things up, not to consciously make up or imagine anything. The trick is to have richer stories by having a richer life—doing things that are worth writing about."

With that, Amelia sighed with exasperation. "So we must suffer day by day just, so you have better stories."

"A better life—or at least the illusion of one!" he insisted.

"And why must you write this story anyway," she continued. "It's just another story about your little humiliations."

"Yes," he agreed, "that's one of the things my stories are about: M and his little humiliations, but maybe there are some moments of triumph too."

2.

Indeed, Amelia knew the Bellagio story all too well. Several years before, M became aware that he had not been invited to a major conference in Mexico City that was to inaugurate and indeed set the agenda for the future of Latin American Cultural Studies. By hook and crook, M succeeded in getting an invite, though without the funding other conferees received. But he had a frequent flyer ticket and the hotel chosen was reasonable in price; and even if it had not been, he knew he must attend even though he had not been and would not be invited to read a paper. A friend did arrange for him to at least monitor a panel so that he had some minimal legitimacy, and off to the conference he went.

M participated as best he could. But at bottom he knew that the others sensed he was a last-minute add-on, who had written nothing in this field to merit an invitation. On this basis, it was tough to contribute without feeling himself to be a buttinsky, and so he was relatively quiet, placing himself as one who had done marvelous things in his sphere, but was now learning and seeking to enter a field in which most of the others present had already produced remarkable things. Of course, it was also true that several other participants were in the same boat as he; however, they tended not to mix with each other but latched on to the more legitimate participants so as not to be part of a definable group of "marginals."

"It's always wrong to push yourself into a conference," M thought, regretting his attendance. "Because you feel like an interloper the whole time you're there." On the other hand if you didn't risk some humiliation sometimes, you would never get into the ring with the participants, never learn what you have to learn, nor meet whom you needed to meet, and never have an inroad into *"le groupe,"* unless you eventually published a book (and how likely was that for M?) which indicated you really belonged there anyway.

Without doubt, his outsider status led him to specific extreme measures that would damage his future standing. So, in an opening dinner when the guests introduced themselves by name, country and university affiliation, he felt the need to be cute by adding a one-line compensatory phrase: *"Soy muy importante,"* he told his fellow conferees. So too, when he chaired the panel, he took his job seriously by cutting off one of the most distinguished and foundational guests for speaking past her time limit. But then came what was a defining moment at the conference, and it was all about Bellagio.

For it so happened that one of the key invited conference speakers was the representative from the great foundation, which had funded the event and the expenses of the key participants. During his discourse, he stated his belief that the participants were opening so many new areas of study that it might well be a wise idea if the group applied to the foundation's Bellagio think tank, where several of the members could continue discussions while writing critical papers on the grounds of the foundation's beautiful estate. The buzz around the room was electric. But M, as he often did, had to put in his two cents that would expose him and probably undermine his hopes and ambitions.

So listening to some of the outsiders rattle on about the greatness of the idea, the significance of such a conference, and (just hinting, of course) the significant contributions they might make to such an event, M, against his better judgment, could not refrain from taking the floor and addressing those gathered.

"I'm sure," he said, "that wonderful things can be accomplished in Bellagio, and I'm sure that all of us would like of course to go." Just the apparent innocence of his expression led at least some people to laugh; but, he added with a wistful tone to his voice, "I'm also sure that some of us will go and … others will not."

At that point his attempt at humor (always a mechanism by which he really signaled his great insecurity, vulnerability, inadequacy and shame) turned into something else. Something like an accusation against the elite group that had initially planned the conference and something like an admission that he was not one of those who could truly expect to be chosen. His words were greeted with a deafening silence, and he suddenly realized he had to rescue the situation somehow. So, still holding the floor, he added, "However, I'm sure that those of us here and elsewhere who don't go will greatly benefit from the findings of those who do."

And it was only then that he sat down.

The conference ending, M met his wife at the airport, and while the most distinguished participants stayed on for a second congress on Free Trade and Culture, they went on their way to on one of his healing journeys through Mexico leaving behind conference injuries and insults to enjoy some days in the sun.

3.

In the months which followed, M, ever the optimist, awaited emails urging all conferees, he among them, to participate in related activities and above all to apply for a special session at the Bellagio think tank. However, even though a prime declared purpose of the Mexico meeting was to set up a "cyber-network" of Cultural Studies thinkers, he never received an email or any other communique. He became convinced that a network had been formed, but that he and other interlopers had been excluded from it. Eventually he heard somehow that a Latin American cultural studies group did in fact visit Bellagio, so he had been right to predict that he and others in his situation were apparently not members of *le groupe* — or at least not in the starting lineup.

It was some years later, and after several conferences to which he was not invited, that M and Amelia indeed stopped by the Lago di Como on their way to a slightly minor symposium at which he was somehow slated to be a significant player. It was early in the morning, but the couple breakfasted, and they were ready to go.

"Let's take a bus trip along the lake," he suggested, "up to Bellagio and beyond." As usual Amelia went along, and sure enough they boarded the bus that went around the lake. Exiting at their chosen destination and, asking for directions, they made their way finally to the grounds of the foundation's famous think tank, proceeding first up to the surrounding gardens, and finally, as the town bells chimed ten a.m., knocking on the door that led to the administrative offices. At last, someone came to the door and M said he was an American professor and wondered if he might visit the estate to get a sense of whether it would be suitable for his future research endeavors. "I'm sorry," the official told him, "but our rules are that only selected fellows may visit our facilities."

"No exceptions?" M asked.

"I'm afraid not," said the official "Sorry, but perhaps you should apply for a fellowship and come back soon." And with that he closed the door, leaving M and Amelia to their own devices.

"Why do you put yourself through such things?" Amelia asked.

"On the chance that such things might work out," he offered, but then he made his admission: "To face my reality as deprecating as it may be, maybe to spur me on too, or at least have the basis for a story. Because if I'd been invited to Bellagio, I'd probably have had no story to write, but the great advantage to my not being invited is that I do have a story to tell."

"A story about not being able to do something," she protested. "But a story nevertheless," he said, almost dragging her to the center of town, where he all but forced her to look at one store after another opening its doors awaiting the first sales of the day.

Somehow M was drawn to the most fashionable shoe store off the central piazza; he insisted they enter and watch as Amelia gravitated toward a pair of red shoes, which he then coaxed her to try on. She could not hide her fascination with the shoes, nor her reluctance at their purchasing something far beyond their means. However, it was clear M would not take no for an answer—perhaps they were far from the top of the line, but they were after all a pair purchased in one of the principal towns of one of Italy's key resort areas. M asked the shopkeeper to help him.

"Bella!" she exclaimed, cooperating. "Perfecta per lei! You take them," she said, "and then you can always tell people you bought them in Bellagio... Look," she said, "They have Bellagio printed on the instep, and look, Bellagio's also on the bag."

"Why not take a picture?" she said, thrusting the shoes in the bag and handing them to Amelia while M took a quick snapshot. Then it was *ciao, arrivederci,* as the couple proceeded to the Bellagio landing dock where they awaited a motorboat that would cross the lake to a second bus that would them back to Como.

It was at this moment of waiting that M, unsure a boat would indeed materialize, was able to make his point in a second exemplary way. "Here," he said, putting himself alongside a beautiful blue poster showing the town and with the words in English, "Welcome to Bellagio." "take my picture with the poster and yes," he added, indicating where she should stand, "with the town behind us." Then he said, "And here, from this angle, with the lake behind us." Amelia reluctantly but obligingly prepared to shoot the final picture, when M raised his fist in victory, *"Veni vidi vici a Bellagio!"* he cried out as she clicked the camera.

"I don't know why you want these silly photos," she said.

"Because they show we got to Bellagio, " he said. "They're tokens of victory."

"Great victory," she answered, "just humiliating yourself again. And who's going to see them?"

"Maybe no one," he answered, "but I'll know about them and they'll be in my story."

"And can't they be in your story without you taking them?"

"Absolutely not," he answered, as the boat arrived and took them out of their misery.

4.

Only a few years later, M and Amelia found themselves at an academic conference in Las Vegas and could not resist a walkthrough of the grounds of the Bellagio. It seemed they entered every nook and cranny of the lush estate, marveling at the crass stupidity of it all. "Don't say I never went to Bellagio," M quipped, and they had a good if painful laugh before moving on to Venice.

That night, Amelia gone to rest; and M, returning to the Bellagio casino, ran into a group of Latin Americans who had been at the Mexico City conference. One of them, perhaps the most famous woman critic in his field, now into her cups, demanded that he show her how to gamble. A bit boozed himself, M could not restrain himself from trying to impress the woman critic who even seemed interested in him (or so he imagined) in ways she had never shown before but that had little relation to his critical prowess or gambling abilities. At one point she berated him for publishing with others and not with her and urged him to send her his next manuscript. He, for his part, knew he would never send her anything, imagining how she would find what he wrote wanting. But here in Bellagio's casino, in these circumstances, she continued to urge him to gamble, and he, caught up in her game, continued to play blackjack with a woman dealer who seemed to pull 20s and 21s out of her hat and soon topped things off with two Ace-Kings in a row. At this point, the famous critic threw up her hands and berated him. "You publish with the wrong people and you're rotten at cards. What are you good at anyway?"

And before he could venture a snappy answer, she walked away, leaving him to play out his last doomed dollars at the casino, leaving him with the knowledge too that in cards as in books, he just didn't know how to play.

5.

So now, lunching in front of the lake, and looking at the streaming sailboats, M once again had the opportunity to visit the Mecca of his frustrated Latin Americanist dreams. He had already submitted his letter of retirement. One of his closest childhood friends had just died. Somehow, he had failed to make a date to visit their most important mutual friend, one who had excelled in his early shows of smarts and who M knew lived nearby with his Italian wife and family, still teaching and growing in reputation as the years went on. M could not help but go over all this in his mind, and finally told his wife, "You know, you're right." I've no right to inflict this detour on you. We'll just go on to Stresa."

"Are you sure?" she said, relenting now that he had apparently made a show of consideration for her. "Won't it ruin your story? I mean, you have to go to Bellagio, don't you?"

"No," he said, "It's not really necessary."

"And you'd still be able to write about returning there?"

"No," he said, "that would go against the rules."

"Then what would you write about?" she could not help asking.

"About not going," he answered, "about not having any reason to go there. About thinking I needed to go and then realizing I didn't have to."

A J Dream

One day M received an invitation in the mail to attend a presentation in Chicago in honor of his friend J's most recent book of poetry, a book beyond his previous works, taking his art to a new level of abstraction and perfection, confirming J's place as a poet's poet unresponsive to latest trends, mapping the J the poet's own ever-higher trajectory even as J the man might be moving toward more profound isolation and yes, death.

M had become used to J's occasional salutary letters which came to him from time to time over the years. Letters in his perfect, disciplined hand, with little content, but with the decorousness and grace of a poet who has much to do or miles to go but takes a brief second to at least give a semblance of communication with a friend. But M had not heard from J in some years, ever since he had sent J and his wife Lois a slim book of stories marking his limited output as a fiction writer up to that point in his life. J had seemingly received M's other recent books with bland encouragement. But this time, J remarked on the book's small size—and perhaps by implication the lack of constant and energetic production or commitment it indicated. After this, there was silence, or worse, even rejection of some of the times he had sought to visit his friend, or even have a drink with him as he passed through town on one of his infrequent stops in or nearby Chicago for a reading.

But now came this invitation, and M was elated, even though he forced himself to acknowledge that it was not necessarily a call to renewed friendship but rather perhaps even an inadvertence generated by the failure to exclude his name from a mailing list. Then too, the message he received was not clear, because indeed it invited him not necessarily to a presentation *by* but perhaps *about* J even when the poet might be tucked away cozily into his Vermont home, writing still a newer set of erudite and esoteric poems while his fans or minions paid tribute to him elsewhere.

What made the invitation still stranger to M was that it was to be held at an African American center on the city's Southside. J was clearly a writer with roots in the African American tradition, but his trajectory had taken him far afield. His writing often seemed to M as if Yeats or Elliot had tried to tell a Black story. Quite decisively, J's writing explored African, Caribbean, U.S. and other roots—even the roots of the slave owner whose last name he bore. Indeed, J had recounted to him the time during a visit to the Edinburgh International Theater Festival and his wife had gone to the house and knocked on the door of the family whose name he bore—*Guess who's coming to dinner*—only to be greeted with high-spirited pleasure by people eager to know their inadvertent relative from the New World.

In their early days, J had taken M through the mean streets of San Francisco's Fillmore District in the late fifties. He had gone with him to a party in L.A.'s Compton ghetto; he had taken M to see Malcolm X, and only months before Malcom's murder, had walked with M through the streets of Harlem, heading south toward El Barrio itself. But that was all part of a past J had for the most part left behind. He had been praised to the sky by one of the gurus of modern criticism. To see that he was to be honored at a ghetto center, that a jazz group would be part of the event, and that the center was named after Paul Robeson all but amazed M. For he remembered taking Lois and J to a Northside jazz club, and there being appalled by the riot breaking out outside the club in reaction to the verdict in the Rodney King trial. J had been offered a position as writer in residence at the University of Chicago; but probably because of the reality of Black America he'd seen in the streets, decided to retreat to his Vermont home.

So, M was surprised and even further surprised when as he readied himself for the trip to the Southside, Lois knocked on the door and told him that J had told her to seek out M to escort her to the event. M did not know how to react. He was clearly going alone; Amelia was gone, perhaps she was in Puerto Rico, maybe she had left him or even left life itself. He felt so entirely alone, and nowhere was the wife of his lost friend, New Jersey Jewish like himself, and his friend's fierce manager-protector, who M blamed perhaps unjustly for being significantly responsible for the loss of his friend. It was she who almost always answered the phone when he called; she who engaged him in prolonged conversation, protecting J from vulgar others such as himself, until begrudgingly letting them speak together a few minutes. He questioned the way she organized his cv. and PR work—as if she were not thoroughly

72

capable in this regard. She probably scoffed at his writing and took offense at his offer to try to get him gigs or even publish a collection of his Latin American and Caribbean-centered poems. Some years back she had told him that the imminent death of her mother, combined with J's prostate problems, would make it near impossible for her to communicate with him in the near future—as if J wrote with his genitals, M mused ironically, or as if that loyal Jewish wife hadn't finally cut them off (what good were they now in any event?).

But reconsidering, going beyond appearances, had she not been subject to J's approval or wishes, tacit or otherwise? Was she not the hard cop, the no to his maybe, the wrong to his right? Had she not taken on this bodyguard role at his bidding?

And now here she was at his door, friendly and even intimate, kissing him on the cheek and gently gliding him out of his apartment as if she were a high school sweetheart taking him to some place where they would share an enjoyable experience in their young lives. At the center, they saw the large poster-like paintings of Malcolm X, Martin Luther King, and towering above them, the larger than life photo of Robeson himself. Looking around at the gathered crowd, M saw old functionaries of the Chicago CP, friends of Harold Washington and other fellow travelers. There were also figures like Mohammed Ali and Richard Wright, Ralph Ellison and even lesser lights left or right like J's old reprobate friends, Donald in Berkeley and Lee in San Francisco. James Baldwin came in for a peak and then wandered off—it just didn't seem to be the right crowd for him.

"Well," whispered Lois, "They've finally recognized him as a Black poet—as if he'd ever stopped being that even as he became so much more."

The evening began with a recording of Robeson singing but then M realized J was not only not there but he would never show up at all, even though he had even sent Lois to bring him. He could not bear her almost flirtatious cuddliness as she tried to all but envelop him in her fur coat and remind him of almost all the New Jersey Jewish girls of his youth.

"J will be very happy to know you came here," she said. "And I'm really happy too."

Suddenly it occurred to M that she had killed J even if he was still writing book after book. He broke away from her and ran from all the Robeson lovers out into the street.

It was very dark, and fog encroached on the street illumination, generating eerie islands of light. M shivered from cold and fear. Suddenly he saw a tall ominous figure enter one of **the** pools, and then as he drew near, he realized that the character wore a trench coat and fedora Bogart-style. And then he realized that the man was black, but though he looked nothing like J, it was J.

"J, you've showed up," M said with happiness and something of reverence. J was after all the writer M wanted to be but could never be.

"Naw," said J in the feigned plain-speech he foisted on one and all as part of his persona as deep poet and regular guy. "You know I would never show up at such a dumb show—

all these dudes sitting around pretending they're there for me when they're only there for themselves."

M knew what he meant, and it certainly sounded like J, but his doubts grew. "J why do you look so different?" he asked.

"To fool these fools," he said, "And maybe you too," he chuckled almost in a whisper. "See, I've gained some weight and got a little darker just to fool these fellows, but the truth is it's still me underneath." And he pirouetted, showing his larger, beefier and yes younger self.

And then M knew it could not really be him, and suddenly J looked like a black version of Orson Welles not as the incorruptible Othello, but as the corrupt Harry in *The Third Man* or the Sheriff in *Touch of Evil*. And M's outrage grew to the size of his fear and yes, his sadness too.

"Who are you?" he asked. "What have you done with my friend?"

"But I am your friend," the figure insisted.

"A friend wouldn't act like this. A friend wouldn't invite a friend to a party and not show up, a friend wouldn't send his wife to deceive and fool his supposed friend. A friend wouldn't send all those friendly letters showing your contempt for me. You are not my friend and you're not J."

"But I am," the figure insisted. "You just didn't know me as well as you thought you did. Good seein' you again," he said, and disappeared into the fog.

David and Jackie

Somehow my son David got a job in Chicago working for a small office dealing with software and compositional and editing problems. He told me to check it out so that maybe both of us could work out of the same office. I called for an interview, made the appointment. The interview was more like a conversation with an old friend, as I found that the editor was in fact a former professor with many publications but needing help with all the requests for work he was getting in. I got the job of helping him, though whether we'd divide the pile of assignments or divide the work on each was something we'd have to explore at some future time.

The important thing is that David and I were there, not with precisely the same hours, but enough overlap that we saw each other daily. The bosses were quite friendly and lax. We had no sense of deadline, or even of tasks to carry out. We found our way into the office at our scheduled time, chatted with the bosses and each other, sometimes managed lunch or after work hookups, even sitting in on the jazz club that was downstairs from the office and was just starting to cook as we finished out our never-too-arduous workday.

The arrangement was so great, and I was so happy we were there together that I was in the best humor I'd been in for years. What happened to David' wife and family was beyond me, but who was I to ask impertinent questions. As much as I loved and enjoyed his family, there was nothing better for me than having my son so thoroughly in my life after so many long years.

Then one day, surprisingly, I received a call at the office from my friend and theatre partner of the late 1960s, Jackie Tubens. I was shocked to receive her call because after a long lapse in communication, I had written her in 1980, only to receive a letter back from her son telling me that she had recently died of a heart attack. I had been shocked by the news because Jackie was so careful about her health and her mother had lived to be well over 90, so I'd never anticipated an early death for her and was always somewhat lax in my communication with her because I always assumed there'd be time for us to catch up. It is true her ideas had become so 60s-radical and her husband so soured on life, that that had put a cramp on our relation. By the time her husband had died, and I'd become somewhat more radical myself, it would have been easy for me to communicate with her. But now I lived in Minnesota, and my life and marriage were not going well, so I didn't want to write her and only did after I'd moved away from wife and son and took on work in Wisconsin and then Chicago. It was then after losing David as someone in my daily life that I decided to write her and received the shocking note from her son. And it was now only after I was fully reunited with my son, that suddenly Jackie appeared out of nowhere.

"You thought I was dead, didn't you? she asked.

"Yes," I told her. "I had heard of Bill's death and when I moved to Chicago, I wrote you, only to have Karl tell me you had died."

"Well, my son was very sick," she told me. "When Bill got sick, Karl took over our mail, and told everyone who wrote I was dead. He even invented a story about me falling madly in love with an L.A. theater director who'd led me on to think he'd produce my plays and sent me scurrying up and down and the freeway from San Diego to L.A. like a young border girl connecting with Hollywood."

"And none of that was true?" I asked, for Karl had indeed written to me about this as the last crazy acts of his crazy mother."

"Not at all!" she said, "I'm still with my Bill, who's recovered and is very much alive; and I've yet to fall in love with an L.A. director, though," she added gaily, "who knows what life will bring."

"Well," I say, "so Bill's ok?"

"Yes," she says, "and he sends his love. "

"Me too, I said, "but where are you?"

"In the same city as you!" She laughed. "We've been here for some time but only heard you were here from your boss—it all came up at a party we went to last week—he's a longtime friend of Bill's. from their Hollywood days."

"I can't believe this!" I said, totally shocked.

"Well it's true! And we want to see you! I understand you're with David, that sweet little boy I remember so well."

"Yes, we're working together—don't ask me how."

"Well," she said, "Some people are coming by for some drinks tonight. Why don't you two come too? You won't believe the crazy place we live in, and you won't feel trapped by us because of the other people coming!" she teased.

"Jackie, we won't feel trapped—it'll be wonderful to see you, and Bill too." So, she gave me the address.

David agreed to join me, so I picked him up in my car in front of our worksite, and off we went to see Jackie and Bill at the hour indicated.

But when we got the address, we faced what seemed to be a wall without doors. We would have driven away, but we saw others parking and approaching the wall. Someone knew the trick and with finger click, a break in the wall opened and expanded until we could walk into a space that was a high-ceilinged but empty lobby, where a speaker recording told us to wait in front of a second door that apparently led to the apartment. I was speechless, but David asked one of the women waiting to enter what was this about.

"It's one of these postmodern entrances, and you need to master the trick click to get access," she replied. "But wait till you see their place—it's a beautiful boat apartment moored on the river but with access to the lake. Whenever we come to visit, we end up cruising past all the beautiful buildings of the city—it's marvelous."

I couldn't help but imagine what fabulous success would have led Jackie and Bill to have such a special place—perhaps he'd finally sold another script to Hollywood after his years of blacklisting and rejection. But I was getting nervous as nothing seemed to be happening. Ultimately, however, the door opened, and the first to arrive pushed their way through. On the other hand, the opening closed, and we were left stranded in the ante-room. I quickly dialed Jackie to explain what had happened.

"You mean the concierge didn't keep the door open for you?"

"There was no concierge—there was no one here!"

"Oh my god!" she exclaimed, "And the worst of it is I can't come to get you because Bill had the boat on a timer and now we've left the dock."

"Well, I guess we'll have to meet some other time," I said, trying to console her.

"Yes," she said. "I'm so sorry! But let me put Bill on."

And sure enough, Bill started talking. "My god there's nothing I can do, and I really was dying to see you! I can't tell you how bored I am in this city and I was hoping we could go out someplace."

I was somewhat surprised by his disappointment and enthusiasm, because my relationship had been more with her than him—he was always so sour, cynical and lost. But I answered in the same spirit. "Look Bill don't worry about it, we'll get together soon. There's a jazz club right down from the office where David and I are working, so you can meet us there, maybe tomorrow night."

"I can't tomorrow," he said. "But some other night!" he said.

"OK.," I said, cutting off the call.

David and I walked back to the car, somewhat taken aback by all that had happened. "Do you think they did this on purpose?" I asked as I began to drive off, "because I lost touch for so many years, and when I got Karl's letter about Jackie's death, I never answered. Maybe they never meant to let us in. And I'll bet he never calls me to hear jazz."

"He probably doesn't even like jazz," said David.

"Then to hell with him," said M. "And all these old memories and relations with people from the one's past."

"But that's where all your stories come from, even if it hurts sometimes."

"Well, at least I brought you to live where I do," M said. "That's something good that came of all this—despite all the frustration and disillusion."

"But, M," said David, "That's as much of a dream as your re-encounter with the Tubens."

"Yes," M admitted. "It's been pleasant to dream it even if it's beginning to hurt now."

III. Retirement Dreams

*T*he Letters

During the last phase of his teaching years, M had to write two evaluations of his students' work. He had to explain why this student had switched from Professor Tomson's class where he was doing poorly, to his own, where, apparently, he was now doing so well. He also had to explain why another student received a decent grade when a review of his work showed that he was a true failure in all he tried. M was able to write the first letter from notes, explaining that his past dealings with the student induced him to listen to his pleas and go out of his way to release him from Tomson's class and accept him in his. He made it clear that he had no intention of implying that he was somehow superior to Professor Tomson nor in any way questioning his colleague's professional capacities—it was just that some professors worked better with certain students, and some students with particular professors—and that was what this was all about.

Time was passing as M wrote, and he knew he had to complete his second letter in a matter of minutes. It was a ticklish matter, because the more he had reviewed the student's work, the more he came to realize that he had somehow overvalued the student's essays and had in effect endorsed and indeed seemed to have praised inferior performance. Accepting the judgment then of his colleagues, he still sought to explain how in given instances, it was useful to encourage students, to somehow give them the confidence to do better, and see if this little strategy might bring out heretofore unseen qualities in certain individuals. He acknowledged that that was a dangerous way to go, that the result might give students a specific basis for complaints and even a lawsuit in which they might be able to bring M's evaluations to the table as they questioned the negative assessments of others. In this respect as in all, honesty was always the best policy, and yet M had made the dubious exception which, he now understood, might prove to be the rule.

It was no doubt painful for M to write this note, to admit to a certain looseness in his academic rigor. But even worse, to confirm out of fear the incompetence of a student whom he still believed had some inner spark that might still have a chance to ignite if he could continue with his studies. But fear was indeed making M's hands tremble, making it hard for him to complete his draft, let alone submit the polished letter. He already knew that there were malicious colleagues who were already doubting his fading competence and even some wondering if there might be some extra-academic and extra-professional reasons (perhaps licentious, scandalous ones) for these two cases, not to mention others they now may be regretting not having acted upon. M knew in his heart that he was innocent, that the problem merely was that he had lost his zest for helping students even as he had gotten older and his teaching skills had admittedly declined. Wasn't all this to-do over these two cases merely a means of trying to pressure him out of his profession? Shouldn't he write a stronger, stiffer, second letter defending his conduct more forcefully and in effect telling his colleagues to go to hell.

He struggled with his notes, tried to rearrange them and write a better explanation. But it was all a jumble on the page, his notes difficult to decipher and written down in kinds of circles so that he had to constantly rotate the sheet of paper to read at least some of what he had written. Matters grew even worse when his chair called him and asked about his progress, scolding him, urging him to finish before the impending time when the committee would meet. So on he went, until the departmental secretary came in and said that people were waiting for his letter and wondering if she might help.

"Yes," he said gratefully, "See if you can read this and put it on the computer, while I draft a final paragraph."

She immediately set to work and tried to transcribe what he'd written, but after a few minutes she stopped, saying, "I'm sorry, but I can't read your writing and what's more the little I can make out is something I could not collaborate in your saying."

"What do you mean?" M all but shouted, offended that, as a relatively uneducated member of the staff, she nevertheless felt she had a right to form a judgment about him. It was after she left his office in trying to hide her tears that he realized he had been unfair to her, that she was right. He could no longer vouch for his words and excuses. The best thing to do was to apologize to the secretary and then tell the committee that he realized there was no excuse for what he had done, and that it might be best if he submitted, at this time, his letter of resignation. He now knew a letter would be received with feigned regret and unstated relief by his colleagues who could begin planning his farewell party, preparing the plaque he would receive and of course, organizing the search they would then be compelled to undertake as they sought to bring a younger and more competent (and, yes, cutting edge) colleague to their program.

Tom and Mary Visit M

Tom and his wife are visiting in Houston. At first, we talked about my townhouse and their own two residential properties in the city where they live; then they both told me that they'd closed on the second property and had brought him some kitchen appliances and utensils that they had thought I might wish to keep in case circumstances so warranted. I went with them to find a pile-up of odds and ends in front of the building where I had my office. I went over the objects with them; and even though I knew they were probably unsuitable, I expressed my eagerness to take them even as I was getting ready to put my basics in storage. Somehow, they disappeared, and I looked for them going from place to place in the building, at last entering a small meeting room. There the Spanish Department was holding a quite elite symposium to which I had not been invited, even though, I should note, I was the outgoing but still active department chair.

Despite some hostile glances, I sat down at the conference table and realized that my recent books were the central topic of one of the famous presenters—a matter which could not fail to flatter me, even if the presentation was part of an event in which my exclusion from the official symposium roster constituted a rather obvious and blatant snub. Furthermore, I must admit that the characterization of my work was not as flattering as I might have hoped for. But of course, even the severest criticism is better than being ignored. Meanwhile I saw Tom's head peering at me from behind another guest. It's also true I recognized hardly anyone from the department except the symposium organizer, so I gathered that this colleague had virtually excluded all the friends I had in our unit. But yes, it occurred to me, that's why Tom was here in Houston, though he hadn't had the heart to tell me—he's here to witness my total negation. And sure enough, when I looked at the famous names on the symposium program, it was evident that he also was not after all one of the listed speakers so that his very presence there was perhaps even more problematic than my own. Growing more uncomfortable, confused and embarrassed by the minute, I somehow found the opportune moment to leave the session, though not without a wave of my hand to the professor who was now aggressively attacking my academic work. I went back to the pile of appliances, and began carting them to my apartment, walking across the campus. I brought them in and started to arrange them for storage. Tom and Mary found me there. We talked a bit and I thanked them with feigned gratitude for their useless gifts, and then they left.

When they were gone, it suddenly occurred to me that maybe they had been trying to send me a message. And perhaps too, the department members had surreptitiously and unofficially invited them for that purpose—that Tom was to confirm the negative assessment of my work and my effect on the department's achievement. His wife was there as a friend to soften the blow I was soon to receive. Perhaps they were not there because they did not wish to give any appearance of being among those involved in what amounted to be a conspiracy.

It also occurred to me that while they had most certainly been provided with lodging, Tom and Mary might have wanted an invitation to stay at my place a few more days, so we could have some friendship time together. I hadn't offered, nor did I suggest we go out to eat, as they had often done with me on my visits to their city. I regretted my inaction. But how could I invite them, when unbeknownst even to my conscious self I had apparently grasped the ultimate purpose of their visit and even the questionable gifts they had brought me? I had in fact prevented myself from tempting them into conflict of interest. Still, I felt ashamed, and tried to call them, but they didn't answer. I felt at a loss, a bit empty and foul. But what was there to do? I just had to accept things as they were and as they were going to be.

2.

It was just when I had literally given up on having any further contact with either of them, that Tom called saying what I'd imagined he would say. "I just wanted you to know," he stated, "that I know you've probably figured out why we're here. And it must seem shabby that we would be involved in this situation, but you should understand that your colleagues no longer back you and they felt that facing this news would be better if we were there to buffer it."

"But why couldn't they have just ended the hypocrisy and owned up to their decision? And how could you let yourselves be party to something so false and underhanded?"

"Because we love you despite everything," Tom said.

"Despite what?" M asked in amazement.

"Despite your terrible shows of poor judgment and your character weaknesses that more than one of your colleagues have noted—and then, if you must know, also, despite the terrible referrals you have made to me over the years that have made Mary and me suffer more than once."

"What referrals?"

"Well you sent us that right wing professor who all but scuttled our projects, until I found a way to get rid of him and his wife who managed to wheedle her way into our program. And then I found out that his leaving your university had meant your getting your job. And then you sent a rave letter that cinched the job for a language coordinator who almost ruined our department, and all because you wanted an opening for a Venezuelan woman you may well have wanted to sleep with. And then you sent us a graduate student who was the coordinator's girlfriend, and who ended up sleeping with a colleague whose wife then divorced him. And then, worst of all, you sent us that Guatemalan novelist you made a hero in one of your books and who then took everything I taught and wrote about and twisted it around into an attack on me and those whose writing I championed."

"But Tom," M answered. "Is that why you and Mary all but insulted me with the obviously useless things you foisted on me? Those are maybe small matters to you, but they sent me a terrible message, I must tell you. Just remember the things I told you and Mary that helped your lives. And remember the other times I helped you in your professional and personal lives."

"Yes," Tom conceded, "I quite remember those things, and they're part of why Mary and I decided to come here, even though it hurt us to have to be the ones to do it. But I want you to remember how I recommended you for different publications and different jobs, and how it was I who recommended you for this very chairship, which has earned you a minimally decent retirement pay, by the way, and why I accepted the role of being the one to tell you and urge you that it's now time for you to leave it all behind and retire as soon as possible.,

"Very good," I said, feeling grateful and grieved at once. "But what's happened is you rescued me only to throw me back now into the hole once again."

"Look M, you went your own way, and that wasn't too bad for you either. And now the real gift that Mary and I can give you is our blessing, so you can go back to the writing career you left behind to pursue one as critic-theorist with which you were never fully happy. This, my friend, will be the best advice I've ever offered anyone, and though it will be a rough road filled with potholes and detours, it will make your final years far less painful than they would otherwise be—and believe me, I promise to help you with all this, until the very end."

"Well, I guess all this is fine, the best conclusion to all," M conceded. "But even if all turns out for the very best, there is one thing, that one night that still taunts and haunts me and will so do me to the end of my days."

"And what is that?" Tom asked.

"That night so many years ago, when you showed up after that conference which opened one of the doors to your breakthrough, and then—" I paused.

"What happened?"

"You, Tom—you ate all my mom's cabbage soup!"

A Useless Man

M faced the fact that his days as professor were quickly coming to an end. The semester was now over, and there was no invitation to continue, no suggestion that he at least give a seminar, do something that contributed to the education of anyone. He spoke to a few younger colleagues in the main office, expressing his dismay at the obvious message that no one valued his services, that had probably been the case for some time, and that might readily apply to the perceived value of his overall career. A few of these colleagues, perhaps appreciative of his better moments and sympathetic about his situation, suggested places where he might apply, but M sensed they were just going through the motions, trying to allay his fears at least until the conversation ended and he finally accepted his situation. And even as they talked, he caught an image of himself in a mirror which was inexplicably positioned to reflect those in the room, and he saw how grizzly and old he had become, how illogical it was for him to seek further work or any further way to validate himself in this life.

M left the building and waited for his wife to pick him up on the street. When she arrived she seemed frantic, saying she needed to look for one of their grandsons whose father had been killed. M wished to tell her of his realization, his sense that his own life was ebbing away. But his wife became desperate and screamed that he should stop thinking of himself and help her. M suggested they should look for Sammy on foot. But she could find no parking place and accused him of trying to deter her search. She followed his lead in getting out of the car, which he then lifted onto a snow-pile. M was surprised by the lightness of the car, especially given his advanced age. But indeed, the object he had lifted now seemed to be a table much like the one on which M was now writing his life stories.

"You see?" said his wife. "Only your stories count and only your wonderful achievements—and now we can't even look for our grandson. You've made everything impossible and useless."

He himself felt he fit her description. "But at least this situation's given me this little story," he mused. Besides, he reassured himself, the grandson would most likely reappear in his own good time. And then he realized, of course, that "most likely" was not quite good enough.

A Post-Retirement Job

Retired now, M returned to his prior home and lined the bottom rows of his bookcase with the fourteen books and the many editions he had published between 1980 and the year of his retirement. Then he lined a few other shelves with the collection of books and journals in which his own work appeared. All this was meant to boost his ego each time he might feel low, to show that yes, he had indeed accomplished something. Even after he had been virtually barred from his career early on and had only found it after years of terrible struggle, only to lose it as we all do if we live so long. His career was not over, he insisted; his books would continue to flow, and sure enough he embarked on one project after another, also waiting for offers to teach advanced seminars and whatever as the days rolled on.

Still no single offer came his way even though he let it be known that he was quite available. And more and more the hours of his retirement which were supposedly freeing him to do more and more work were becoming a burden that was difficult to bear. Why don't I seek a job—a regular job somewhere, at least until an invitation to teach materializes. And then, sure enough, a friend found him a lead—to work as a pourer and server in special spinoff parties at a fancy downtown hotel restaurant. He quickly made an appointment and went for his interview, which turned out to be more of a hands-on tryout rather than a standard Q and A.

"The thing is," said the lead interviewer, "You have to be fast and attentive on this job." You must be fast and ready with glasses, with ice, and above all with the stirrers. I can't stress how important the stirrers are. In fact, the way we do this is we insert the sharp end of the stirrers onto the skin of our arms, like arrows ready to use. We always keep some four or six ready even as we get the glasses and put ice in at least some of them as we attempt to stand ready for each order and refill."

Without explaining further, he lightly jabbed the first stirrer into M's arm; and M, showing his willingness to cooperate, inserted three others, each causing him more pain and even some bleeding, as he attempted not to wince or groan.

"That's fine," said another member of the team. "You'll get used to this if you stay on the job." "If!" said still another member, almost laughing. "And be sure not to stain the table cloths or leave your body fluids in any drinks!" said still another.

Sure, enough the customers now came into the room and M raced to fill their orders, putting ice and serving the proper drinks, removing stirrers from his arms and placing them in the glasses. He rushed to insert new stirrers and fill new drink orders even if the process itself seemed to slow down the service more than help it.

"You're doing fine," said the lead interviewer during a break in the action, "But don't just stand around after you've done the service. See if they need more ice, urge them on to their refills, make them truly happy so they'll leave big tips and rebook with us."

So, M struggled on with renewed resolve, suffering however, each time he had to jab the stirrers in his arms, cognizant that he was indeed dripping blood and that someone might protest. But no one seemed to mind, as the party continued, and he began to feel ever weaker even as he increased his attentiveness and worked ever harder. Soon his interviewers were gone, and the partiers began to depart. A moment came when he was alone in the room, alone with his sore and bleeding arms, to say nothing of the pains from his flat feet and sore ankles. And he suddenly realized he'd been taken, used as slave labor by a bunch of swindlers who'd no intention of ever hiring him again, and who'd even pocketed his tips before going off—no doubt to celebrate their exploitation of still another poor beggar like himself.

M in the Audience

M found himself at the back of a large auditorium at a large and prestigious university listening to a new rising professor expounding his central views to an audience which included M's brother-in-law and several intellectuals many of whom M had debated at academic conferences over the years. M was wearing a shirt that he could not keep in his pants and was hanging over the sides of his unpleasantly paunchy belly. He was surprised to see that the speaker, so far away, also had his shirt untucked, though in in tune with current fashion, he wore a slim-fit sport jacket over the shirt. M was disconcerted by this partial similarity with the speaker, even though he knew the effect was quite different in his own case. He was above all impressed by the talent and profundity of the speaker so grounded in the richest levels of cultural theory as well as matters of ontology. Yet he found it strange that, ever so often, amid his deepest observations, the speaker would interject a phrase like "Did you see that movie? It's one of the best." Or "That hit song, it's just great."

M interpreted such interjections as parodies of contemporary discourse, so influenced by texting, tweeting and other short cut reductions of communication. It was as if the speaker were acknowledging that even the most avant garde kind of intellectual discourse meant nothing in a contemporary post-cinematic world governed by electronic media and simulacra in its many guises.

M considered this strategy of interjections a clever ruse, perhaps beyond the majority of the speaker's intended listeners, but not beyond M of course. Indeed, M was on the other hand also surprised to hear what he believed were subtle references to his own work, as if the speaker knew M was there and had decided to pay homage to him in ways most others had never done, never recognizing his contributions which however bypassed and surpassed by younger and more recently emerging thinkers, still provided links from a past point of stagnation to whatever point of progress had been reached from a previous period to the apparent time of breakthrough in which the new generation of scholars believed they lived. Considering this sense, it even seemed to him that the speaker had spotted him in the crowd and had, in his own discrete way, acknowledged M's appearance in the audience, even going so far as to wink at him, or at least so M interpreted a gesture, though clearly it might have been just a kind of reflex action, some squint or twitch that M was incorrectly interpreting. And yes, there seemed to be something perhaps ironic, sarcastic or at least sardonic in the apparent citations from M's work, as if the clichés about movies were making fun of M at least as much as they were of contemporary mores and discourse. And once M realized this distinct possibility, he began to feel a sense of outrage about what he considered the injustice being done to him first by a recent generation which, usually without acknowledgment, had built on his work even as they had all but forgotten him and a still newer generation which only honored him through a pastiche of parodic rerfences, if any one remembered him at all.

And yet now as the speaker kept on, M realized that regardless all the parodies he seemed to be hearing of his own words, still the over-riding and dismaying truth he had to face was that try as he might, he hardly understood a word of what the professor was saying. He wondered if it was a problem of hearing not uncommon to those of his age. But then he realized he was hearing and understanding every word clearly, but he simply was not comprehending the meaning of the words taken as a whole; he simply was unable to understand the perfectly clear verbal enunciations he was hearing.

"So, it's come to this," he mused, "people in what was once and very recently my profession are now saying things that are completely beyond me." And he cursed himself for having grown lax in his work, for not caring enough to keep up with new theories and new knowledge, as if he wanted to continue playing without doing the necessary work, as if he had some right to his jealousy of those who had kept on and moved ahead, when he had done nothing to stay in the game.

And now the truth was outing and M was caught in a trap at least partially of his own making; and what dismayed him all the more was his fear that, since his words were, he thought, being echoed even if in parody, the speaker might wish to acknowledge him and indeed ask his opinion on one point or another in his talk when as M knew, he understood nothing and, if allowed to speak, he would expose his nakedness for all to see. As the talk went on, M realized that his fearful thoughts were further preventing him from hearing anything the professor said—which meant that he would be even less likely to be able to respond to any question or comment by the professor than he had been before.

"What can I say when he calls on me?" he asked himself, and he knew from the continued citing of his work that it was more and more an issue. "And yes, the movie was tremendous," the professor intoned.

And with that, M felt the growing prostate-driven urge to go to the bathroom and yet he knew that any move he made to get up and leave might lead the professor to diverge from his ordered discourse, to finally recognize the man he was citing. And so indeed M held his seat, repressing his urgent needs, and dreading what seemed to be turning into horrendous endgame. For, as it often occurred to him, the need to repress an urgent urination urge all but inevitably led to his falling asleep. And this, given his fear that the professor might call on him at any moment, led to an ever-greater fear that he would indeed nod, only to be caught, as it were, and as many so phrased it, with his pants down. And this fear of humiliation before a new generation of scholars, who would only have even more reason to pass him by, was beyond what M could bear. The solution lay within his reach because he always carried a can of double expresso to deal with the almost compulsive, driven urge to sleep. But that antidote had its terrible side effects, including, the most terrible of all—that sudden need to race to the bathroom that was the very effect his sleepiness might in some sense be attempting to prevent his experiencing. So there, caught in his catch 22 or 3, M was almost reeling from the multiple effects of his situation, while the professor went on citing and probably mocking him, while adding once again for god knows how many times that this movie or that song was oh so fine.

And now, it became clear that the professor was truly winding up his talk and M's terror grew that he would be called upon and that his ignorance and academic emptiness would be revealed. So what could he do as the professor moved toward his final remarks, but stand up and move, not toward the men's room, but down the aisle toward the speaker, to mount the platform.

And at the moment of his final word which M could almost hear and time, even if he could not understand a bit of it or grasp its internal movement or logic, to say to the audience as he indeed did say, "Wasn't he wonderful?"

And then, turning to the surprised professor, M whispered, "Wonderful, Professor X" pronouncing the professor's name as he embraced him while simultaneously waving to the audience and repeated his name, following it with "Wonderful—and the movie was just great!"

At which point the audience broke into applause, and the professor looked at him and asked, "But who are you?"

And M replied, "But don't tell me you're going to pretend not to know me, after citing me all afternoon."

"But I don't know you," said the astonished professor, as the audience continued applauding, "I've never seen you or heard of you before in my life."

*T*he Unannounced Professor

I am trying to confirm the arrangements for a talk I'm supposed to give on globalization and the new left turns in Latin America. I talk to the secretary of the program that's invited me to speak, requesting setup details, but no one's available. Even the professor who's invited me is nowhere to be seen. Nor is there an event scheduled, even though I have my plane ticket and letter of invitation indicating my hotel and other arrangements.

"Must've fallen through the cracks," the secretary tells me. But when I press her on the matter, she says, "The person who invited you's been removed."

"Really?" I ask.

"For making unauthorized commitments without consultation or commitment from the faculty."

"I see," I say. "But surely it has nothing to do with me personally."

"That may be so, but then again some may feel you were part of a conspiracy to appropriate departmental funds."

"Which explains the boycott of any arrangements for my appearance..."

"Could be," says the secretary.

"Well, can I speak to the acting chair—or the dean?" I ask.

"You certainly may make an appointment, but both are out of town, and won't be back for some days."

"Well then, who can I talk to?"

"Me, I suppose. Everyone else has washed their hands of the matter and has indicated they're not available."

"Even Dr. Fraughtson, who's co-editor of a book we did."

"He's also been discredited in his scholarly work and took an option to retire. Quite a scandal. It's a wonder you didn't know about it."

"Well, yes, I've been getting lax over time; I failed to renew my subscription to *The Chronicle of Higher Education.*"

"Well we must keep up, mustn't we?" said the secretary, almost sneering at my limitations. "But don't worry, your hotel reservation's good for the night, and if you really want to give a talk, you can draft a flyer and we'll get it out so that maybe some interested souls may see it by tomorrow."

I knew I should leave in answer to the situation in which I had been placed. But I had come a long way; I had my books to sell, and maybe I could get an audience after all. So I took off my jacket, asked for paper and pen and asked the secretary to find an empty classroom and a minimally adequate time slot, and started drafting the flyer.

"Here," I said, handing the secretary my draft plus a photo of myself and my last book cover, hoping I would get my opportunity despite all.

2.

The next thing I knew, I had called my son David and told him about my situation. He immediately took a plane and found his way to my hotel, ready to help me, he said, in any way possible. It soon became clear, however, that he was not there to help me prepare but to pack me for departure, "before there was any further humiliation."

"But I've made the flyer, the secretary's sending it out on her listserve... Maybe some people will show, I'll give my talk and I'll even sell a few books.

"This is nonsense," he said. "There's too little chance of anything here except an undeserved blow. Let's get out of here first thing in the morning."

So he didn't help me prepare, and I waited for him to sleep, while I drafted a special opening and close for my talk which I hoped would please my audience. When I awoke, David was gone—though he left me a note saying he was going off to visit a new friend he'd made on the plane. I waited for him and a call from the secretary to see if all was ready for my talk. I breakfasted, read over my text, packed my books for the presentation, and was ready to take a cab to the designated lecture space when David reappeared.

"I think I've made a real friend," he said. "I left my mailing address, and I'm sure we'll be in touch. So now let's get out of here."

"No," I told him. "I'm going to give my talk whether you're with me or not. You've done nothing to help me as it is."

"But dad, aren't you happy I've made a friend?" David asked, glaring at me. "In spite of your academic careerism which devours everything."

I couldn't bear the accusation another second. "I have to give this talk," I said, "whether you're with me or not." And I took the cab now waiting for me.

3.

When I got to the lecture site, I was stunned by the elegance of the setting and of the many people attending. Apparently, the secretary had done a marvelous job in selling this event to an impressive crowd of people. Drinks were being served by tuxedoed waiters, and I must admit to taking and drinking more than one. However, as time went by, I became increasingly nervous first because no one seemed to acknowledge my presence, and second because I suddenly found myself to be all but naked, my fat pudgy body and even an outline of my privates available for all to see.

"But how has this happened?" I cried out to myself, "and how have I let this happen and why has my son left me in such a state?" And I suddenly spied a table with a large, regal-looking gold cloth, and I immediately raced toward it and wrapped it around me, hiding my near-nudity which at least some people might have noticed. But to my great relief, nobody commented on my previous appearance, but many

ooed and ahed at my new-found elegance, as most of the crowd suddenly seemed to notice me and burst into applause as they saw me enveloped in what must have appeared to be papal attire.

The applause spurred me on and made me forget my recent state of utter embarrassment, humiliation and abandonment. I took out my prepared comments and made ready to read, when David entered the room and went to my side, shouting "No! No! My father, an undoubted expert in his field, will not read today in protest against the way the former department chairman and his invitation to speak had been handled."

Soon some chanted, "Let the professor talk! Let the teacher teach!"

Then they were joined by others who shouted, "Down with censorship. Down with the academic dictatorship."

And in all the hubbub, David steered me out the door and into an awaiting cab, which took us to the departmental office, where I picked up a bag I'd left.

"How'd the talk go?" the secretary asked.

"As well as could be expected," I answered, and made my way back to the waiting cab.

"Dad," David said as I got in the car, "I think maybe you should give up on the lecture circuit."

I knew that if he'd have let me speak, I could have won over the crowd with my brilliant insights into the most contemporary complexities facing our field of study. But I also understood that he was trying to help me even if making a new friend was at one point more important than that goal. And since he was my son, I let him live in what to him must have been an illusion which made him happy. He had too few friends, and it was important for him to make new ones if he could, especially given how little time my career ambitions had left for him as he was growing up. As for me, I knew I would give future presentations no matter whenever or what.

One Intellectual and Another

1.

One night M caught up with Albert Einstein and as Jew to Jew, he praised him for his great contributions but complained bitterly first that his work had led to so many dead in Japan, and second that he had done nothing to help the Puerto Rican people as they came to the New York area even as the Manhattan Project advanced. "

"What are you talking about?" the great theoretician exclaimed, apparently considering the second matter more important than the first. "It was I who recognized my key theories lodged as elegantly as $E= mc^2$ in the crypto-Judeo/Caribbean writing of the iconic New Jersey poet William Carlos Williams. And it was I who insisted that Princeton hire the Puerto Rican literary scholar, Arcadio Díaz Quinones!"

M was taken aback by these revelations, and his own failure to have recognized the role of this great intellectual. However, this apparently trivial failure on M's part was only the prelude to another, more profound one.

2.

By what seemed to him a very calculated move, M and his wife of 30 yeats had been invited to sit at the head table at a high priced fundraising dinner held by one of Chicago's key Puerto Rican centers. The dinner honored a radical Jewish intellectual whose work, while never touching directly on things Puerto Rican, was clearly free of Zionist baggage, was at least indirectly anti-colonialist and implicitly honored the Puerto Rican community and its leaders.

The purpose of the dinner was to build future cultural and fundraising projects. As M understood the matter, his own future role did not escape the center's decision makers who viewed his Jewish roots, his Puerto Rican marriage and his own intellectual work as the basis for his possible elevation in his more advanced old age to a level which, while never in any way reaching the exalted status achieved by the current honoree, could somehow enter into what might be construed as a nevertheless significant place in the construction of future relations.

M distinguished between being used or useful in a decent cause. He could not help but feel honored, even if on the spot and without prior preparation time, he was asked to say a few words introducing the honored guest.

"You probably know more about him and his work than anyone here," Pablo Medrano whispered to him. "I wonder if you could say a few words about him—kind of place him for people here who hardly know anything about him."

"I'll do my best," M said, "though a prior invite might have led to a better intro," he could not help adding. Of course, it occurred to him that someone else had been assigned this role and had failed to deliver or maybe even show up; and so he was probably being asked out of desperation, and his help might well be remembered with some gratitude. In any event he immediately began to rehearse in his mind some of the connections that made the guest a figure of immense importance to the world, and in that context to the Puerto Rican community. So he was perhaps readier for the role he was being asked to play than he himself might acknowledge.

Once he agreed to do the honors, he watched Pablo go to the man of the hour and whisper to him, gesturing toward M presumably as the man who would introduce him. The honoree nodded his head with some apparent enthusiasm gesturing in M's direction, and then whispered something that Pablo felt the immediate need to communicate to M. "He's very pleased, he says honored, that you'll introduce him. But he suggests that it would be best if all concerned would not reference the Jewish connection."

M nodded his head in a way that communicated his understanding and compliance with the venerated intellectual and he received acknowledgement in return.

"He also asks if you could somehow keep a mental record of what you say, and what he says—to jot down the key ideas at least so he and others could have some future record."

"You can tell him I'll do my best," M affirmed, nodding his head as if to communicate again with the elder figure, even going so far as to mimic writing down notes the way one might do in requesting the bill from a waiter. Again, the man of the hour expressed his gratitude, this time going so far as to put his hand over his heart.

"It seems he's no better prepared than I am," M whispered to Amalia.

"Do you really have to prepare to give these little talks?" she asked, playing out her usual role as a deflator of intellectual pretensions.

It is of no significance to this story here what was said by introducer and introduced—or even what was said in the introduction of the introducer. What is important is the fact that the following morning M went about his task of recapitulating all he and the venerated guest managed to improvise, paying special attention to capturing the order and flavor of the latter's discourse, and putting it all on a pen-drive to deliver to him as soon as possible. Later that morning he called Pablo who thanked him profusely and gave him the honored guest's phone number. Making the call, he finally got through and indicated he had a draft of his discourse notes which he would be happy to hand-deliver and go over with him whenever it was convenient.

"Can you come over now?" the elder man requested, with some excitement.

"Certainly," M said; and taking a few minutes to round out his own introduction, he left the house and drove over to the address indicated, arriving in less than 45 minutes after the telephone conversation.

An aide of the honored intellectual answered the door and ushered him into the old man's studio.

"Ah, I was afraid you got lost," said the intellectual, apparently anxious to see the texts at hand.

"Well here I am and here are the first drafts of the texts," M answered, handing his host the pendrive.

"Thank you so much," he said, "I can't tell you how much I appreciate your way of humoring an old man. And here," he said, "have a seat and join me for some coffee and a light snack."

"You didn't have to go to the trouble," said M.

"The least I could do for the work I've heaped upon a man at a time in life when you probably have a million things of your own and deadlines to meet every day. "

"Well," said M, submitting to the gesture for him to sit down. "it's very nice to hear that from you with your own work in full swing."

"At my age, you know that every hour can be your last, so you really try to prioritize and eliminate more tasks than you take on—or, as in your unfortunate case, to delegate some of them to someone foolish or generous enough (and it sometimes comes to the same thing) help out. In any event, I wanted to take this opportunity to meet you because while I confess I haven't read your work, others tell me that it's more than good, and apparently in tune with some of my own."

"Well, I certainly agree with many of your ideas and they've probably affected mine, to the degree that I've felt it right to cite you quite often, so readers wouldn't think I was making claim to ideas or expressions that were yours. But beyond that, there's no way my own feeble efforts can be compared with yours, no way that – "

"Yes, yes," said his host with surprising impatience just when M was obviously going to sing his praises. "That's fine," he said, patting M on the shoulder. "No need to rehearse the wonders of my books—I know their limitations all too well. What really intrigues me and what I really wanted to know and what led me to ask your collaboration with me, is what is this group that invited me. What interest they could possibly find in anything I've written, because to tell you the truth, I've racked my brain and can't think of any reference I've made at all to Puerto Rico, the Caribbean, Latin America, Latinos or anything that might directly relate to their world—except a few words I might have written about the evils of slavery and racism."

M was amazed that the venerated speaker hadn't gone to the trouble of finding out about the group before agreeing to accept an honor which at least implicitly linked his accomplishments with the group's identity, achievements and aspirations. He was also surprised that he seemed oblivious to the kinds of connections he had sought to make in introduction the previous night. It was not lost on him that his host still had not asked to go over the pendrive texts with him. Still, he felt compelled to answer. "Questions of slavery and racism are much to the point," he insisted, "especially when they are part of a discourse centered on human liberation and creativity of all kinds. For how such questions can be explored, or goals be pursued in a colonial context?"

"Is that how you see my work?" the host said with amazement written all over his face.

"That's how I saw Eros and Civilization, The One-Dimensional Man, Soviet Marxism and your later, shorter volumes"

"But I didn't write any of those works!"

"What!" M exclaimed in amazement. "You didn't write— "

"No," said his host. "That's what struck me as totally absurd with your introduction. You attributed to me a whole series of works and ideas—not to say a life story—that had nothing to do with me and everything to do with Herbert Marcuse, a radical but elitist intellectual with a completely different trajectory from mine."

"And you're not Herbert Marcuse?" asked M now astounded. For hadn't the event been announced for weeks as a dinner in honor of Marcuse? Wasn't this the man he'd introduced?

"Marcuse's been dead for years," his host said. "And I'm not quite dead yet."

"Then who are you?" M asked with the deepest sense of bewilderment and humiliation.

"I'm Studs," his host said. "Studs Terkel—I was the one they were honoring and the one you were supposed to introduce. You're much younger than me, but you seem to be completely lost. You need to see a doctor, and right away. "

And with that, his host led him out of the study to the front door of his house. M all but staggered to his car and made his way home, wondering what he would tell his wife, wondering why neither Pablo nor any one from the Puerto Rican center had said anything to dispel his misunderstanding, but knowing that his future with the center would never be what he had imagined. But then, what could someone in his state of mind be said to know about anything?

The Impossible Interview

(Note: *Really, Amelia didn't go with M, but the plaza and kiosk were quite alive, the coffee quite good, and the interview turned out to be quite possible and successful. Things were quite different in the dream M had the night before.*)

As part of a retirement project I'd developed on Puerto Rican artists with Chicago connections, I'd arranged an interview with Felipe Cordero, a Puerto Rican painter now 85 years old who'd worked for over a decade in the Windy City so many years before. I heard of him through a mutual friend, got his telephone number and agreed to meet him on Wednesday at 10 a.m. at a well-known Plaza Palmer coffee kiosk in Caguas, the town he'd chosen for what might well be his final home.

Amelia said she wouldn't go, but when I woke up in the morning, she was already dressed. "You've overslept," she said. "We have to leave in a few minutes if we're going to get there on time."

I was happy she'd decided to go, so we could make a day of it after the interview. Everything always went better when she was with me. I dressed quickly, but had trouble finding my shoes. Luckily, I'd set my GPS the night before, but when I finally found my shoes, I knew we could get there on time only if I skipped the coffee she'd prepared for me. I really hadn't wanted to meet him in a public space, but he'd insisted;

and without my morning coffee I was still groggy and now looked forward to the expressos the kiosk was known to serve. We got to the plaza in no time. There was the kiosk, and there was Felipe Cordero, tall and robust for his years.

"I'm glad you got here on time, he said. "Because it turns out that a talk I was supposed to give late this afternoon, they've rescheduled for this morning—right now, so our interview will have to wait until then."

I was eager to order my coffee, but he was urgent we leave immediately, escorting us down a side street, to a large building which seemed to be some kind of meeting hall for Masons, Lions or who knows what. There was **an** ante-sala with lots of tables and chairs. And then we entered the main space, which turned out to be a large auditorium but with a floor that was not raked and **with** folding chairs instead of fixed seats. Most of the seats were already taken by countless numbers of students and their teachers, it seemed. It looked like everything was set up for no little chat but for a big program that would take some time.

"Damn," I whispered to Amelia. "This will take a few hours, and then it'll be time to lunch. Who knows when I can begin my interview and when we can get back to San Juan. By that time, I'll be totally exhausted, so there goes our day."

Sure enough, Felipe approached us, his presentation notes in hand. In a flash I could see that he had several pages of dark, single spaced text with lots of side notes.

"My god, this is going to take a long time. And all this without my morning coffee. Maybe I should tell him we'll come back another day."

"But we're already here," Amelia said. "We might as well stay."

"Damn these artists! You can never count on them keeping to any schedule," I muttered.

I went to the bathroom; but when I came back our seats were taken, and Amelia was nowhere in sight. I suddenly saw that most of the available seats were arranged in relation to given tables, and I found myself approaching a group of young people who were laughing and talking away, almost completely in English. "Hola!" said one of them. "Have a seat."

No sooner had I accepted the invitation when someone on the raised platform started another group of students singing a big militant anthem-like song, filled with words like *Lucha, resistir*, and the like.

"What is that song?" I whispered.

"That's the anthem of Caguas," a student told me. "But most of the music will be from Connecticut. "

"Why Connecticut?" I asked. "Because it's near New York, just like us."

"But we're in Puerto Rico, near Venezuela," I insisted.

"Yeah," he said in English. "But our music's more like lower New England."

"Connecticut hip-hop or *reggaeton*," said another, as the kids laughed.

Suddenly I saw Amelia motioning me with a pair of chairs, and I went to her to sit down. A speaker began his introduction and went on and on as Felipe waited. At a certain point I could stand it no longer, got up, and without saying a word to Amelia, left the hall and went back to the famous kiosk still hoping for a cup of its even more famous coffee. But the place had closed down—even the chairs and tables must have been packed away. I decided to explore the area to see if I could have better luck elsewhere. Walking across the plaza, I finally entered what turned out to be a large and elegant bar which looked impressive enough but turned out to be populated by the poorest of the poor, several of them obviously drunk and maybe in the final stages of alcoholism. I bolted from the bar and looked around the square, realizing all the buildings were in terrible shape, decrepit, abandoned and falling apart.

"Maybe the people have moved to Chicago, now that Cordero lives here," I thought. "Or maybe they've all moved to Connecticut—or Orlando.". It was so depressing seeing what had happened around this once new central plaza, now in ruins like so many others on the islands. "And this is even before the Hurricane," I heard myself say. "I'm so glad my grandson's left and is now trying to make a life in our city." And, once I thought these thoughts, I had had enough—and I decided to return to the hall as soon as I could.

On the way, I saw a grey, emaciated man, his ribcage bones all too visible, lift an even more emaciated man on his shoulders and finally place what looked much like a grey cadaver on top of his own sack of bones. He came very close to me and I could smell the stench of decay and rot, so I started walking faster to avoid a collision.

"Don't worry," the man said, sensing my alarm. "There's nothing you can do about it , so you might as well accept what comes your way," he went on in a voice that came from some deep and lost place. It soon turned into a screech that pierced M's ears, even as this half-cadaver/ half-live man walked on to an abandoned lot where he proceeded to dump the body from his shoulders and then followed that body into a pit that seemed to be a grave for countless souls like himself.

That did it for me. I now raced toward the meeting place again, and entered the ante-sala now filled with a large group of people having a meeting of their own—or was it a wake? I passed them and entered the auditorium where the conference continued. Then I made my way to where I'd last seen Amelia, but she wasn't there, and I realized suddenly that I was walking around in socks, and I no longer had my shoes. Had I left them somewhere in town? With the half-cadaver/ half-live man? Under a chair? The conference continued. But all I could think of were my lost shoes. Where could I find them? Or Amelia? Or the artist? Or anything?

The Scene and the Dream

1.

One night, watching *Henry and June* in a downtown Chicago movie house, Amelia leaned over toward M and whispered, "Don't turn your head or do anything crazy, but I think that's Plácido Domingo watching the movie with his wife."

M quickly turned in the direction Amelia's body language had indicated—and sure enough it was Plácido Domingo, wearing a black leather jacket and sitting with a woman who might well be his wife, trying to watch the movie, but huddling more into his jacket and even tucking his head into his companion's shoulder. More and more people began to follow M's lead, leaning over to assure themselves what others were telling them—that they were indeed in the presence of the man who was at least the second most celebrated tenor of his generation.

Soon, perhaps embarrassed by their obvious gaggling, M and most of the others who had been caught up in the glory of the great singer's presence, now returned to the movie and its intriguing story of artistic creation, rivalry, male and female, eroticism, love and madness. As the film came to its laborious end, the audience exited, and many of the over-fifty crowd of men made their way to the restroom before leaving the theater. After a long wait M finally found himself before a stall unzipping his fly and trying to urinate, when a man in a leather coat came to stand next to him. This time, trying to restrain himself as he had not done at the earlier moment, M still managed to confirm that it was the great singer who had joined him at the stall. It was difficult for him to urinate under the circumstances, and he only succeeded when the singer had finished his own business and left the bathroom.

Finally relieved, M zipped up and washed, making his way into the lobby. "You'll never believe this," he told his wife. "But Plácido Domingo was pissing right next to me..."

"And...?" she asked.

"He's a great singer," he said, as they left the theater.

2.

His grandsons' ever so advanced and cutting-edge elementary school in Minneapolis proudly announced to a thrilled community that famed opera singer Plácido Domingo would lead the student singing group, along with volunteering relatives, in a concert performance of one of Verdi's most wonderful operas. M accepted an invitation directly from his daughter-in-law to participate in the event, and he flew up from Chicago to the Twin Cities to help enhance the performance of his grandsons in the upcoming concert.

There was no time for M to rehearse with the group, but his son David had told the conductor about his father's fine voice and his early experience in singing groups; and the conductor met briefly with M to discuss his assigned role. "I want you to be our guest's shadow, adding a further comic dimension to his overall performance by echoing and indeed parodying his phrasing and (let me be frank) his at times bombastic style."

M hesitated, but the conductor sought to allay his doubts. "I'm sure this will be a sensational touch, which our honored guest will end up thoroughly enjoying. I can just see him over-riding your parodies with some of his own—of you and maybe of himself as well And I believe the students and their parent volunteers will be overwhelmed by what occurs!"

M could only be flattered by the conductor's unusual proposal. He had always secretly wished to show off his fine voice and indeed his acting verve which he had hidden from the world most of his life. Here, at last, was his chance thrown right into his lap. However, he worried and wondered about the conductor's use of the word, "overwhelmed"—about whether this dream opportunity might not distract from the performances of the kids themselves, his grandchildren included. But what was to be done? He did not want to disappoint and perhaps prejudice the very conductor whose job it was to bring out the best from his students and the other volunteering relatives.

So all was now set for the exceptional performance.

The students gathered on stage and sang rousing versions of the National Anthem and the school alma mater. Then the volunteering relatives came on stage to enthusiastic applause, which rose to a roar as lo and behold, the great Plácido made his great entrance. The tech person started the recorded opera music, and the chorus began with a sequence of trills, leading to a brilliant series of runs performed by Domingo and then echoed by the chorus of singers, who reached a peak and were silenced as the conductor signaled for M to begin his parodic echoing of Domingo's solo.

At first tentative, M found himself getting into his role and drawing on other performances by the second greatest tenor of the previous generation of opera singers. That second greatest now looked somewhat surprised and perhaps dismayed or displeased, as the conductor had given him no inkling of this new and wonderful last touch to an already magnificent performance design. Still, he calmly waited as the chorus started again, leading to his second solo outburst, again met with applause and then seconded by the chorus, and finally again, by another comic and now booming parody of Domingo's already booming style. This time the audience applauded with great verve; and M, instead of being pleased, felt a rush of anxiety for his having gotten carried away and perhaps having insulted a wonderful singer and at the same time distracting from the other performers and above all his grandsons.

Meanwhile, Domingo, somewhat unnerved, signaled to the conductor to have the tech person pause the orchestral music as he delivered an elaborate and masterful parody of the parody made of his singing. And then he transformed the parody into a broader one highlighting some of his most inspired bravado performances so that the students and all present who were not already standing rose to their feet and thundered forth their seemingly interminable applause, shouting Bravo! Bravo! Until the great Plácido urged them to simmer down; and only when having silenced one and all, he now spoke into a microphone that suddenly found its way into his hands.

"Ladies and gentlemen," he said with his English which mixed accents of Castillian and Mexican Spanish. "It has been an immense pleasure to come and sing for you at the invitation of my dear friend, and a wonderful musician, I might add, your esteemed school conductor. However, when I was asked to sing with your students and volunteers, I had no idea that my playful friend had a further trick up his sleeve and inserted a second soloist into the mix. Let me tell you I have never been so surprised in all my years of performing, first by the audacity of my friend and then by the remarkable quality of my shadow or better put my echo or virtual double as it were, who has acquitted himself with such consummate skill here on this stage."

At this point, this second greatest singer of his generation, motioned to M, who shyly, though now somewhat proudly moved to the great man's side, and, overwhelmed himself, fell into the bear-hug of an embrace that was offered to him, only to hear Domingo whisper, in his best English and in the midst of their most intimate moment, "Don't ever think of doing something like this again, you piece of shit."

It was at this point that the conductor, sensing he had gone too far, came to the side of his two soloists and thanked the great singer for submitting to his joke. Then, with a sweeping gesture, he publicly praised M for helping, and all but dismissed him from the stage, sending him toward the wings under a hail of applause, as the conductor then explained that the performance would now continue as initially planned. At that point Domingo resumed his position as soloist, the students and other volunteers (except M) prepared to start; and with a wave of his baton, the conductor recommenced a concert now unburdened by the presence of M and all the high jinks attendant to his compulsive necessity to call attention to himself.

M watched and heard all from his relegated position in the wings. It seemed his glorious moment was fading by the second, and a sense of regret grew within him. Feeling he had been drawn into an impossible situation, he nevertheless glowed as he heard the small but lovely solos sung by the children and, marvel of marvels, his grandsons, as he joined in cheering the great singer and the other performers while the concert drew to its close.

After the performance, his son and daughter-in-law came backstage to greet their sons and tell them how well they had done. But the boys insisted it was M who had stolen the show.

"No, boys," he said contritely, "I sang loud, but you

sang very well—and that makes an enormous difference."

"Damn," said David when he was alone with father. "You always make a big hit when you come to Minnesota. Next time if we get together, I think it should be in Chicago."

David's wife said nothing, but she nodded her assent and pursed her lips into a seemingly vague smile as she and all the performers made their way out of the theater.

A Hotel on the Borderland

He had made all his plans for a two-day stay in a border town where he was supposed to evaluate a college program. The hotel was secured and he had all he needed so that nothing could go wrong. But when he finally pulled into his room, he found his wife's daughter, almost his daughter, sleeping in his bed.

"What are you doing here?" he blurted out.

"Well, I was at a convention down the street, and it got pretty wild, so I thought I'd get some rest over your place. "

"I'm sorry," M said, "but I didn't even know you were coming here this weekend, and I don't know how you knew I'd be here."

"My boys found it through your emails— "

"But how did they do that?" M asked, nervous about this invasion of his privacy and this disruption of his arrangements.

"I don't know about that, but I know they did it. And here I am."

Before he could answer her, large numbers of people began filing into his hotel room, which seemed to grow in size, though not in proportion to those entering. He seemed to know some of them, perhaps in relation to his evaluation duties. But many seemed to be strangers, perhaps attendees of his daughter's conference, who had somehow followed her to the hotel.

Among the crowd, was one obvious hooker who whispered to him, "Are you the one who called me saying you wanted me to come over?"

"What are you talking about?" he barked at her, enraged by her impertinence, the inference she seemed to wish onlookers to draw and the scandal she seemed intent on creating, especially in front of his daughter. But then she seemed to get lost in the crowd and was perhaps out the door, though who knew if she left alone or with one or more of those in attendance.

Then, just when the room seemed to be most fully packed, the people began to leave, going down the stairs and flowing onto the streets where they mixed with the gaggle of prostitutes who generally pedaled themselves in the area. A few of them approached M, one even signaling toward his crotch. But he quickly retreated back to his room to avoid any appearance of impropriety.

The room was back to its normal size, but suddenly it occurred to him that his almost-daughter might still be there. At first, he found no sign of her; but taking more precautions, he moved the blankets and sheets, and there, as if buried in them, she lay sleeping, dreaming and snoring away.

"Seems like I paid the money for the room, and she's the one reaping the rewards," he said to himself, relishing the irony even as he felt thoroughly alarmed at what she might tell her mother (his wife, after all) about the kind of place she'd found him in on his business trip.

He just stared at her but soon she awoke and immediately went to rinse her face and, yawning, she prepared to go back to the convention. "Great place you've chosen—a great setup," she said to him with a grimace that was almost a sneer.

And at that point a feminine figure appeared at the door. But it was not one of the women he'd seen on the street, but rather it was his wife, who came into the room, as casual as can be. "I came to the convention with her," she said. But now I want to know where we're going for lunch?" she asked.

"Well I wish I'd known," he said. "But I do know a little bistro not far from here," he answered, as if all was back to normal.

"I hope it's still in business," she answered.

"Me too," said the daughter, as the three got ready to leave the nest. He somehow felt some tinge of loss, but of course he felt relieved. How could he bear being without these women in his life?

_M_ Loses His Wife

M and Amelia endured the plane trip and even enjoyed the last phase which took them directly over the amazingly tall buildings they could see out their window and come dangerously near as the plane passed through the downtown and made its way toward the airport. "Look," said the pilot, "some of the tallest buildings you can imagine and whoops! See how easy it might be to get too close **to** them!" he joked, as he made it seem to barely skirt one and then ride up another until the plane lurched up and beyond as it made its final downward swoop toward the smoothest of landings.

It was almost 7 p.m. when the plane touched down; and by the time they made their way to the hotel room, they were too tired to do more than unpack, have dinner in the hotel restaurant and head back to the room for a quiet, restful night before their tourist adventure began. Strangely, watching TV with his wife, he sensed her somewhat in tune with him as if she might have some faint stir of desire. But as in many other such occasions, M did not pursue what might or might not be hints, for fear of experiencing another frustrating and saddening rejection, as had been the case on countless prior occasions. Besides, at his advanced age, he was in no great need to pursue what might be only the slightest spark that might turn to ashes at any moment.

What did bother him in all this was that he felt somehow unwell, as if he'd eaten something disagreeable, something that wasn't quite right. And indeed, the discomfort persisted to the point that he decided that if he felt the same way in the morning, he might well have to inconvenience their first day of tourism by a trip to a local clinic to seek a cure for whatever might be affecting him.

Sure enough, the discomfort deepened into a kind of nausea and he finally had to admit it to his wife that he wasn't feeling well and needed to vary their itinerary to find some medical assistance. The hotel staff gave them instructions in how to arrive at the clinic of their official doctor and called ahead to make an appointment. Somehow it was impossible to find a taxi, and no one at the hotel was free to take them, so that M and his wife found himself [themselves?] on a bus heading toward the clinic. To M's surprise, he watched as a rather surly man struck up a conversation with his wife and she took out a card from the hotel as they persisted talking in whispers, until the bus stopped at the indicated location, and M all but pushed her toward the door.

"Oh, here's our stop," she told the man as M kept prodding her along with is right elbow. "Ask for Amelia," she said loud enough for all, including M, to hear, as they exited off the bus.

M felt a growing sense of outrage until he finally turned toward her and asked how she could have flirted with a stranger right in front of him and in these circumstances.

"What's wrong with you?" she answered. "He just

wanted some information. And would you prefer I spoke with him behind your back?"

"I can't believe you," he answered, and he could not resist giving her a slight punch in the arm to register his sense of outrage and betrayal. "And this happens when I'm not feeling well and can't defend myself. "

"And I suppose that's my fault too," she answered, with a certain insinuation that left him mute. They entered the clinic and soon enough he spoke to the doctor.

"Probably just jetlag and indigestion," he said. "But let's take a couple of tests. We can give you the results within the hour."

His shots taken, M returned to the waiting room, where he found his wife engaged with another man, this one seemingly suggesting sites for them to see, but leaning toward her, and she toward him, in a way that seemed more than provocative. The man was going on about the beauty and size of the skyscrapers and other buildings of the city—some being longer horizontally than those that rose vertically over everything.

"You should really visit them, one by one," he told her, and it was clear she was quite impressed.

M found himself interrupting the conversation with a brusqueness that was not his norm. How did this man know the relative sizes and qualities of the buildings? Was he some expert or someone who took advantage of a husband's health problems to impress the husband's wife, when the husband would no longer be in full command of his faculties. Too much a gentleman to enter a dispute with a husband who was clearly blind with jealousy, the gentleman made his retreat, but not without leaving his card with M's wife who seemed quite happy to receive it. When he left the room, M began to upbraid his wife again, wondering what was wrong with her, how she'd become as she was now becoming.

"And what do you want?" she said. "How long has it been since you looked for me and tried to win me, and you expect me to sit by forever watching you spend our money and risk your own health and mine on the first whore you can find in your path."

Shocked, M was about to answer when he was called by the one of the health workers and told that his tests had turned out negative, but that he should get the pills prescribed by his doctor at the pharmacy on the corner. M was confused. He knew of course that negative was positive, but he experienced little sense of relief, but rather a growing, deepening sense of anxiety as he led his wife from the office, and promptly arrived at the drugstore. Soon enough he had his prescription, took his pills and was now ready to show his wife around the city—and show her first hand all the verticalities and horizontalities, the positivities as well as the negativities, so precisely but somehow ambiguously characteristic of this most premeditated of cities. The only problem was that in this great city on the very edge of the world, his wife was nowhere to be found.

The Sculpture

In Memoriam:

José Emilio Pacheco,

Carlos Montemayor,

Carlos Monsiváis,

Octavio Paz,

Carlos Fuentes,

Juan Rulfo,

Most recently, Gabo

And most deeply, Λ. Kerlow (RIP)

Also:

For my friend, Evodio Escalante,

And for Elena Poniatowska.

For months, M lived with one central obsession—that he had somehow broken or defaced a small but valuable sculpture that had been given to him to hold in safekeeping by one of the best-known novelists of the Americas.

The sculpture was a bust-like stylized profile by a respected Mexican modernist artist who somehow thought to honor his country's famous narrator by giving him a representation of his country's greatest poet. On first discovering the rather obvious damage to the piece, M realized he was in serious trouble with his integrity and whatever might be left of his good name at stake. He didn't know what to do other than to hide the piece in his closet. He subsequently moved from his home city and his long-standing university position to a far less cosmopolitan city and place of work. He changed his cell-phone number and even his clothing style; he shaved his beard and only published his articles and books of criticism in obscure venues he knew would draw scant attention. But somehow, he knew that all this would not be enough; and so he could not be totally surprised when, after all his feeble efforts, this very day, he received a call from the famous novelist's secretary. She asked if he was indeed M and if he could arrange for the return of the sculpture in time for it to be the centerpiece of the novelist's seventy-fifth birthday celebration.

M had written some books of literary history and just one slim and unnoticed collection of fiction. He was therefore not surprised but was of course irritated by the fact that it was the secretary and not the novelist who had called him. He was above all dismayed by the prospect of his disgrace—so much so that he claimed to be someone else and said he'd pass on the message. Immediately after the call, he found the piece, and uncovered it, hoping to see it, somehow, in perfect condition— as if his having damaged the article had been a dream. But there it was, jagged along the lines of breakage, destroyed almost beyond recognition.

Try as he might, M could not quite recall what had caused the damage—whether it had been unintentional or otherwise—if the sculpture had been maimed and battered out of envy, resentment, or anger, or if, as he might hope (was it indeed possible?), the damage was really the fault of someone else. He couldn't even remember what the sculpture had looked like and how it might have been altered. Try as he might, he could not recall the most pronounced detail, even as he saw points of breakage and somehow knew it had not been like this when he had received it.

M imagined that it probably irked the novelist that a sculpture made to honor him was not of him but of a national figure who for years had kept the novelist in his shadow as a prime spokesman for his country's literature and culture. The idea behind it all, M surmised, was to recognize the novelist for his somehow having reached a level that perhaps most, if not entirely, approximated that of the poet. If so, maybe this would explain why the novelist didn't want to take the sculpture with him on his travels, and why he had left it with M, since he considered the gift to be an underhanded insult best relegated to a dark recess of what must inevitably be the drab apartment of a somewhat obscure critic and sometime writer. In this case, M 's being entrusted the sculpture might itself have been more of an insult than an honor.

But M wasn't sure of any of this, and it occurred to him that his memory and sense of judgment were failing. Perhaps, he thought hopefully, this could be the excuse that would extricate him from the shame of his disgraceful disfiguration of an important piece of work. But then M realized this was no way out, because it left him exposed as a washed-up, senile figure in the face of the world. As horrible as it might seem, wasn't it better to be a kind of Erostratus, a destroyer of icons and wonders, than a useless old man? Or, was it possible that both interpretations could fall on him as his shame became public?

Then he thought, with the kind of magical thinking of a child who accidents in class and closes his eyes hoping the smell and stain will go away, that all he had to do was lay low, not respond and maybe he would never be called again. Of course, the way to make that dream take place would be to cut off his phone completely and disappear from the obscure city and school where he had come to hide. But that would leave him without an income, and he'd **have** no one to turn to, his wife having left him some time ago, his one child having gone off to who knew where and all his friends alienated and, in some cases, deceased.

What could he do? He began to consider pursuing some of the more extreme alternatives but then his phone rang again, and he blocked his impulse to answer. When it stopped ringing, he waited for the signal that a message had been left. It was Ambrosio Escalera, a well known literary critic, telling him he'd heard that M was on the verge of giving the sculpture to the famous novelist. He asked M if he might accompany him to what seemed might be a significant public event from which, M surmised, the critic thought he might otherwise be excluded.

Then came another call, this time from a glamorous woman free-lance art critic. M feigned the voice of a butler only to hear her insist on calling him by name and asking him, with a glint of suggestion, for a personal interview in relation to this great upcoming ceremony. Then as if that were not enough, there was a knock on the door, and a delivery boy presented him with a package which proved to be the galley proofs for a book on the novelist which opened with a few pictures including one tagged blank space that was marked, *"Photo of award ceremony: Presentation of sculpture of great poet to famous novelist. (Piece possibly presented by M—find out who and where he is and arrange for photo op.)."*

The situation was impossible, and M had no one he could turn to, no one he could talk it through without risking exposure, ridicule and worst. He felt utterly alone, and the ruins of a once mildly happy and successful life were plain enough for him to see. He sat at his desk, staring at the objects and photos about him. And there, lo and behold, amidst ex-wives and lost loves, M saw, staring back at him, the framed snapshot of his slightly mischievous and only recently deceased friend Martín. He lifted the frame and stared into and almost through his friend's large, smiling, reddish and impudent face, and the devilish glint in his eyes. M realized suddenly how much he missed his wicked friend, what a brother and bother he'd been. Staring at Martín's face, M suddenly trembled and dropped the photo, so that it clattered on the desk, upsetting several of the other objects, and sending not a few along with it to the floor. M saw that the photo glass was now cracked, with the break line cutting across Martín's face. And it was at this precise moment of his most extreme feeling of loss and desperation, from the very bottom of his all but emptied out sense of being, that it dawned on M (was it a repressed memory suddenly visiting upon him?) that it was not he. Of course, after all, how could it be he? but rather his ever-too-playful (and now ever-so-sadly but perhaps conveniently dead) friend who had been the culprit in this matter and the source of his deepest anxiety?

Martín was a doctor who also passed his free moments writing stories and drawing pictures. It especially irked M that this man dedicated to the healing arts was more creative and better read than he, a professional scholar and writer who had always devoted himself to literature. Indeed, Martín was a minor celebrity of the great city from which M was later to flee, a man invited to all openings who in turn frequently held parties for visiting celebrities. Such was the case of the famous novelist on one of his visits to the city, one of the three times M had personally sponsored and hosted him. Finding his apartment inadequate, M felt deeply humiliated as he was virtually compelled to ask Martín if he could use his friend's apartment as the site for a party in the novelist's honor after his public presentation. So it was that there, in Martín's apartment, the novelist was sitting at a desk and signing copies of his latest book for an interminable line of admirers. "Doesn't all this signing bother you?" Martín asked the novelist. "Maybe I could sign some for you," he quipped. "With love and admiration." The novelist laughed and said, "Why no, I can handle the signing" and then he added, "it's always a great pleasure to greet my public."

M found this answer pretentious and pompous, and so did Martín, who commented on it and all the people fawning over the famous novelist in his apartment. "This is the last time I'll hold one of these soirées," said M's talented friend on this night some months before he died, when, as M now realized, Martín began to say goodbye to what had been his life. Another farewell on that road had occurred when on preparing to leave the city, the famous novelist had received the gift of the sculpture from the respected artist but burdened by the luggage required for his book-signing trip, asked that M keep the sculpture until further notice. But, the severe modesty of his apartment also meant that M was in no position to give the sculpture its required security. A few days after the novelist's departure, he now remembered, he had brought the statue to Martín's house for safekeeping as he went off on what he claimed was a little speaking tour of his own, to present his latest findings on some obscure writer of whom the great poet and famous writer had probably never heard—and perhaps with good reason.

M remembered Martín complaining that the novelist was really beyond words, pawning off a mediocre work as a masterpiece and entrusting it to a man who had no clue how to deal with it and would be foolish enough to think it was worth keeping or feel shame about if he failed to do well by it. In fact, Martín railed against the novelist for his arrogance and his pretensions in writing so many words and novels when he was not that talented or wise after all. He attacked the novelist's ever-so-correct politics, which won him high-priced speaking engagements, abundant book sales, and enthusiastic plaudits—especially from certain people who wished so much to be counted among those opposing their own country's policies concerning its "distant neighbor" and Latin America as a whole. He went so far as to remind M that the novelist had once declared that another, less urbane writer from his country, who had only written two slim volumes, was the utmost writer of his generation—although even here, Martín considered this all a pose to win the novelist added admiration.

All this said, Martín took in the sculpture, and it was only on his sudden death that M retrieved it, wrapped in a red towel, and brought it to his home. Just was it then that, as best he remembered now, the piece slipped from his fingers and hit against the desk and was only saved from falling by M's trapping it against the desk's edge. At this moment, opening the towel, M found the piece broken and at this point too, he made matters worse by propping the sculpture on the table, discarding the tiny chips and attempting to fix what could not be fixed.

But M now recalled that it did occur to him then as it did now, that perhaps the near fall of the piece had not been the cause of its breakage and deformation and that it was not he, M, but none other than Martín himself who had damaged the piece before M had opened it. After all, the slip had not been severe, and as always, his fixing efforts were tentative and feeble. It was Martín who indeed prided himself on doing outrageous and unheard-of things. And M now could picture his friend avenging the novelist's pompous behavior and pretentious comments by doing something to the sculpture. An inventive amateur artist himself, Martín would have been quite capable of working over and in fact parodying the original piece until it became a virtual mockery of the novelist and probably even the poet as well.

Looking at the sculpture now, once again, M was impressed by the power of the broken image. Evidently it showed all the signs of his friend's handiwork. But undoubtedly it was better than the forgettable original he had received from the novelist—a tribute to his friend's outrageous character but also his excellent taste and creative power. Now looking at the piece, he decided that what had happened was nothing for him to be ashamed of after all and that he deserved recompense for his months of agonizing.

So it was that, phoenix-like, M garnered his courage and called back the novelist's secretary to inform him that he was well up on the issue at hand and was quite ready now to return the sculpture. The secretary then asked him how he might retrieve the piece, and M said, "I will return it the evening I present it to him on his seventy-fifth birthday. "But the novelist has asked for someone else to present it." "Then tell the novelist that I shall present it to the presenter," M said, now with some courage and resolve, "at the ceremony," he insisted. "Very well," said the secretary, "I shall so inform him of your suggestion." "It's not a suggestion," M was shocked to hear himself say. "It is how it shall be if it shall be at all."

And so it came to be. M called Ambrosio Escalera and invited his ever so eager friend to attend the ceremony with him. He called the publisher of the book-in-progress to confirm that he would be available for the required photo shoot. He called the glamorous freelance critic whose alluring questions led to a provocative interview which appeared in the local press and even circulated in other newspapers throughout the Americas and Europe. He called the secretary to confirm the hour, place, proper attire and overall schedule for the now widely announced event. He had his tux cleaned and bought a special box for the sculpture. He even arranged for a limousine that would take him and Escalera to the event in style.

And so it was. The limousine, large, stark black and portentous, M made the desired impression, and he was called to the stage to bestow the sculpture on a celebrated chronicler who'd been chosen to present it to the novelist. He shook the celebrated chronicler's hand and even took the opportunity to squeeze the hand of the novelist who seemed somewhat taken aback but was of course quite gracious. Then with the shortest speech possible he expressed his sense of honor at having been entrusted the piece and now handing it over to he who would hand it over. He did add a line, however, to express his sorrow that the novelist's host on a recent tour, a man of notable talent who had indeed helped with the sculpture and improved upon it, he added ever so casually, had since passed away. The chronicler/celebrity, giving one of his acidic and witty commentaries, compared the famous novelist with the incomparable poet and then presented the box to the novelist who drew out the sculpture and held it up for all to see. The crowd buzzed with excitement as the piece emerged—there were oohs and ahs and then a round burst of applause.

At the reception which followed, the celebrated chronicler, who was also known as a connoisseur and collector of Mexican art, examined the piece and declared (though in the sardonic, parodic tone all his own) that the respected sculptor had never done anything better. The sculpture was an extreme example of the tension between modernity and postmodernity in their most urban and urbane modes, in which the creative tension between the great poet and the famous novelist, had found its full expression. Poet and novelist posed as boxers in a faceoff before their great fight, as everyone laughed and applauded, and the flashbulbs blinded all in attendance.

A major writer known for his Zapatista sympathies mounted the stage and began to sing a ditty in honor of the occasion; and Escalera, seizing the moment, all but ran to the piano to give him back up.

"This is a memorable event," said a major poet, who attended. "I hope we'll remember it. But will we be remembered? The whole thing is a circus," he concluded.

"What?" a listener asked.

But the poet said he couldn't recall.

"The women remember what's most important," said the most famous woman writer in attendance, as she recorded all that was said, and took notes on what was implied.

In the corner, a novelist from the south who was even more renowned than the famous novelist kept his distance from the local guests as he dreamed of making a film out of the story he was already writing in his head about this festive evening (but another, not he, wrote the story).

Then the glamorous and indeed lovely freelance critic approached M and asked him what he had meant by saying that his friend Martín had somehow improved on the image. She punctuated her question by poking him gently in the ribs, and adding "are you sure you weren't the one who improved it?"

M sidestepped the questions saying it was only a manner of speaking, a figure of speech—a matter which he would be happy to explain in greater detail if given the opportunity. The famous novelist and guest of honor came over to personally thank M and greet Escalera. "I want to thank you for your care," he said to M. "I knew I could count on you," he said pompously. "And how nice of you to come, Ambrose," he added, citing himself, perhaps with a touch of irony aimed at the critic.

M and Escalera left the party elated; they shared a drink before going their separate ways, the limousine dismissed, and each of them staggering home in a separate direction, though sharing in a state of drunken exaltation. Some days later M began dating the glamorous, lovely and ever-more erotic freelancer with whom he came to share more than one secret; and soon after that, he finally published his long-delayed second volume of stories, including one called "The Sculpture." It was well received by a small but select group of critics, one remarking that it was reminiscent of the posthumous and soon-to appear collection M had arranged of his friend Martín's stories and pictures, And another, indeed Escalera, noting that as a whole M's book represented a near-break (or was it a still another crack?), with respect to previous writing and surpassed even the work of a writer whose two short books the famous novelist had confessed were a more significant contribution than his almost thirty novels of production.

As the months went by, the great poet died, much missed and eulogized, perhaps most thoroughly but also most sardonically, by the celebrity-chronicler-connoisseur-collector. Strangely enough, the respected artist, and then even the sardonic chronicler-connoisseur-collector also died, to the great dismay of their many friends and admirers. The novelist-singer-*zapatista*-supporter died, as did the memorable major poet of limited memory, remember? The famous novelist continued writing novel after novel and gave speech after speech, though some argued that he was already a kind of ghost awaiting his final exit. And then he too passed away. And soon afterward, so did the novelist who was even more renowned than the famous novelist.

As for Escalera, he seemed to come into his own in a series of telling essays about each of the lamented icons; and with them gone, his own stock seemed to increase so that he did not have to squeeze his way into any literary events and was often invited to speak. Indeed, some came to claim however erroneously that he himself was the true author of "The Sculpture."

According to Escalera's account and that of others, M was left saddened by the loss of the people who were so central to the world he had known so long; but, almost all agree, he could not help but feel his spirits rise by the day and week. First his glamorous freelancing lover produced a book that was even more praised than his own; and to his surprise, he took pleasure and pride in her success, without a trace of envy. Then too, he began working on a novel he himself believed could be his masterpiece—though in his newfound romantic entanglement and his bourgeoning happiness, so late in life, he realized it didn't matter or mean too much if he finished the novel or not.

*E*pilogue

Night at the Crossroads

Things always happened at this crossroads., to which he returned again and again. This time he was distracted and didn't notice when the others departed for the next town, where they'd agreed to stay. The ticket-seller made it clear: he'd missed the last train to that place, and he'd have to spend the night where he was waiting for transportation in the morning. It no longer made sense to go where they'd gone; instead, he should make straight for the next place on their itinerary. Or even the location beyond that one so he'd be sure not to trail behind, also though it might mean a long, tedious wait until he came together with the group and Amelia.

The critical thing was to get a place to sleep and wake up in time for the connection to the place he'd decided on. That wasn't so hard, because he'd stayed at a hotel here before and he could now go to it, find a light meal nearby and then get to bed early enough to be ready to go in the morning. But somehow, he couldn't find his way to the hotel, and he saw no other hotel wherever he walked—nor a cab, nor a policeman nor anyone to give him directions. Nor did he find a restaurant, nor a bar to have a drink.

Not knowing what to do, he found himself walking in circles brooding over his situation and wondering how he had gone wrong. Why had he allowed himself to be distracted in the first place? Had he wished to escape Amelia? And was this the crossroads town he'd been to before? Where was the hotel? The restaurant? What could he do now?

If only someone would appear to give him a point of reference or refuge, but no one appeared, nothing happened; and he reached the point where the only logical thing for him to do was to return to the station and, bearing the cold, get through the night and then take the first train going where he'd hoped to go. But now he couldn't find the station, even as he wandered from place to place. As the night air grew colder and he had no idea where to go. So it went as the night bore on, so it had gone on in his other visits to the crossroads town. And soon it occurred to him that he had never visited this town before, that there was no group that he'd become detached from, nor was Amelia part of the group, nor would the group or she go where he'd been planning to go. In fact there was no such group, nor a place, nor an itinerary of which that place was part and to which some hypothetical or purely invented group or wife would be going. And indeed, he reluctantly had to realize that all of this was about nothing, because he had gone and would go no place, that he was part of no group and had no love and that all of it had been some kind of fabrication out of the total emptiness which he had to acknowledge was his.

But even this realization could not stop him at the crossroads, but would push him further along, remembering and dreaming, trying, however briefly and trivially, to make something of even the shortest and most deformed, truncated and blasted of all the dreams and scenes of his all but ended life.

ABOUT MARC ZIMMERMAN

Marc Zimmerman is Professor Emeritus of Latin American and Latino Studies at the U. of Illinois in Chicago (UIC); and Spanish and World Cultures and Literature Sections of the Department of Modern and Classical Languages at the University of Houston, where he served as chair (2002-2008); he was also active in Midwest Latino community organizations for over three decades; and he has served as Director of Global CASA/LACASA Books (Latin American and Latino/a Cultural Studies and Activities Arena—now LACASA Chicago) since 1998.

Zimmerman earned his B.A. and M.A. in Creative Writing from San Francisco State University, studying fiction and playwriting with Walter Van Tilburg Clark, Mark Harris, Ray West, Herbert Blau and James Schevill. After serving as a lecturer of World and Ethnic literature at San Diego State University for four years, he earned his Comparative Literature Ph.D. at the University of California at San Diego, studying with Fredric Jameson, Claudio Guillén, Herbert Marcuse and Carlos Blanco Aguinaga.

Following a year teaching English at the U. of Michigan, Ann Arbor, he worked in Minnesota migrant and Latino organizations from 1975-1979; he served as a senior advisor and lecturer in the Literature section of Nicaragua's Ministerio de Cultura in 1979-80, worked as interpreter for U.S. Health

Service at the Cuban Refugee Center in Wisconsin (1980), and then served five years as Coordinator of UIC's Latino Cultural Center, 1980-85. Over the years he taught at the Universidad Autónoma de Nicaragua, McGill University, and the Universidad de Puerto Rico; he also taught mini-seminars at la Universidad de los Andes, Tucumán, Argentina, and la Universidad de Madrid. The recipient of Fulbright, Rockefeller and other major awards, he served for several years on the Fulbright Fellowship Selection Committee; he served on the Caribbean Literature section for Cuba's Casa de las Américas Prize in 1994. As a member of the Latin American Studies Association, he co-chaired the Central American Studies group, and chaired the Culture, Politics and Power group, while serving in Latino and other groups as well.

Many of Zimmerman's articles have appeared in major journals; and he has written and edited some thirty-five books, mainly on general theory as well as on Latin Americanist themes. His books include *Lucien Goldmann: El estructuralismo genético y la creación cultural (1985)* and the seven-volume series, *Pre-post and Post-Positions* (2005-2009), including five English-language volumes on socio-literary theory, on modernity and politics in Europe and Latin America, and a two-volume Spanish language sequence on post-modernity and globalization in Latin America, *El momento fugaz* (2007) and *América Latina en el nuevo [des]orden mundial* (2009). Probably best known as a pioneer in Central American Studies, he has written *Literature and Politics in the Central American Revolutions* (with John Beverley-1990), *Literature and Resistance in Guatemala*

(2 vols.,1995), Literatura y testimonio en Centro-América (2006), and *Goodbye to Political Economy in Central American Cultural Studies? Searching for a Method* (2017).

His Latin and Central Americanist co-edited books include *The Central American Quartet* (collage histories of poetry and other discourse modes portraying the histories of Nicaragua, El Salvador and Guatemala-1980-98), as well as a series of nine works exploring Latin American Cultural Studies in the age of Globalization (2004-2011)— all co-published under the aegis of LACASA, and with two volumes recently re-published on line in the distinguished Alter/nativas series at Ohio State University.

Furthermore, Zimmerman has established a large body of work on Caribbean and Latino culture and literature, including two books, his much-cited *U.S. Latino Literature* (1992) and *Defending their own in the Cold: The Cultural Turns of U.S. Puerto Ricans* (2011*)*, awarded Honorable Mention for the Puerto Rican Studies Association Frank Bonilla Book Prize and a Hermandad Prize, from the Instituto de Puerto Rico in 2012. A new volume on Chicago Chicano writing should appear in 2019. In addition, his co-edited cultural studies volumes include *Processes of Caribbean Unity* (1983) *Globalización, nación, postmodernidad. Estudios culturales puertorriqueños* (2002*)*, *Ir y venir: procesos transnacionales entre América Latina y el norte* (2007), and *Orbis/Urbis Latino: Los "Hispanos" en las ciudades de los Estados Unidos* (2008).

In recent years, Zimmerman has developed work on Chicago Chicano Writing and, above all, a series of interviews and related materials dealing with Chicago Latino (but mainly Mexican and Puerto Rican) art. These efforts are registered on his website www.lacasachicago.org; and he has recently donated an extensive installment of his art-related materials to the Smithsonian Institution, which staff is in the process of organizing as a component of its its Archives of American Art Project. Based on this ongoing work, Zimmerman has thus far published several articles, as well as three texts centered on Chicago Mexican artists José Gamaliel González (2010 and 2013), Aaron Kerlow (2015) and José Guerrero (2016). However, Chicago Puerto Rican art is the subject of his continuing research and the theme he proposes to develop in a series of presentations for this coming year.

Recently returning to his first love of creative writing, Zimmerman has also been developing books of "memoir fiction" (related life-based stories, dreams and fantasies organized into novel-like structures) touching on Jewish, Italian American, Mexican/Chicano, Central American and Puerto Rican themes — with several books in progress, but four already published, including *Stores of Winter* (2005), *Martín and Marvin* (2016), *Lines on the Border* (2017), and *The Italian Daze* (2017), an Italian-language version of which, *La penisola non trovata: I giorni italiani di un viandante perduto*, was published in Milano by Greco e Greco and presented at the Torino International Book Fair in May 2017. Additional volumes are on their way toward completion.

Most of Zimmerman's books are listed with http://amazon.com/author/marczimmerman; several of his most recent essays on Chicago Latino art and literature, as well as some of his stories, may be found in the Chicago Latino online journal, *El BeiSMan*, to which he is a regular contributor (http://www.elbeisman.com/busqueda.php?q=zimmerman).

Married to Esther Soler from Quebradillas, Puerto Rico, Zimmerman divides each year between the island and the Wicker Park/ Humboldt Park area of Latino Chicago. He has recently given talks on Chicago Latino muralism at Dartmouth College, U.C. Berkeley, UCSD, and Purdue University, Calumet; and he has done readings from his fiction at bookstores and libraries in Berkeley, Los Angeles, San Diego, and Chicago, as well as Milano and Torino, Italy.

85585498R00102

Made in the USA
Lexington, KY
02 April 2018